The Life-Changing List

An emotional, uplifting new duet from Scarlet Wilson and Kate Hardy

The lives of Darcy and Felicity Bennett have been at a standstill since losing their beloved sister Laura five years ago.

But Laura had suspected this would happen, so she'd arranged for her solicitor to give them both a bucket list to bring the sisters back together and help them sort out their lives.

Join Darcy and Felicity as they take on the list— and find two handsome companions to help them find joy in life again!

Read Darcy's story in
Slow Dance with the Italian
by Scarlet Wilson

And read Felicity's story in
A Fake Bride's Guide to Forever
by Kate Hardy

Available now!

Dear Reader,

When I was asked if I would write a duet with fellow author Kate Hardy, I jumped at the chance.

When I first started reading Harlequin Romance novels, Kate was one of the first authors I read and loved, alongside Caroline Anderson.

I've been so proud to join them in writing both Harlequin Medical and Romance books.

Writing a duet with Kate is fun. Plotting our sisters' stories and brainstorming together, having little aha moments and forming our bucket list that shaped the stories just made everything pop for me.

Here's hoping you love the stories as much as we do,

Scarlet Wilson

SLOW DANCE WITH THE ITALIAN

SCARLET WILSON

Harlequin

ROMANCE

**H Harlequin®
ROMANCE**

ISBN-13: 978-1-335-59674-1

Recycling programs for this product may not exist in your area.

Slow Dance with the Italian

Copyright © 2024 by Scarlet Wilson

All rights reserved. No part of this book may be used or reproduced in any manner whatsoever without written permission.

Without limiting the author's and publisher's exclusive rights, any unauthorized use of this publication to train generative artificial intelligence (AI) technologies is expressly prohibited.

This is a work of fiction. Names, characters, places and incidents are either the product of the author's imagination or are used fictitiously. Any resemblance to actual persons, living or dead, businesses, companies, events or locales is entirely coincidental.

For questions and comments about the quality of this book, please contact us at CustomerService@Harlequin.com.

TM and ® are trademarks of Harlequin Enterprises ULC.

 Harlequin Enterprises ULC
22 Adelaide St. West, 41st Floor
Toronto, Ontario M5H 4E3, Canada
www.Harlequin.com

Printed in U.S.A.

Scarlet Wilson wrote her first story aged eight and has never stopped. She's worked in the health service for more than thirty years, having trained as a nurse and a health visitor. Scarlet now works in public health and lives on the west coast of Scotland with her fiancé and their two sons. Writing medical romances and contemporary romances is a dream come true for her.

Books by Scarlet Wilson

Harlequin Romance

The Christmas Pact
Cinderella's Costa Rican Adventure

Harlequin Medical Romance

California Nurses
Nurse with a Billion Dollar Secret

Night Shift in Barcelona
The Night They Never Forgot

Neonatal Nurses
Neonatal Doc on Her Doorstep

Marriage Miracle in Emergency
Snowed In with the Surgeon
A Daddy for Her Twins
Cinderella's Kiss with the ER Doc

Visit the Author Profile page
at Harlequin.com for more titles.

This book is dedicated to my fellow author
Kate Hardy, who always motivates me to
work hard and write better stories

Praise for
Scarlet Wilson

"Charming and oh so passionate,
Cinderella and the Surgeon was everything I love
about Harlequin Medicals. Author Scarlet Wilson
created a flowing story rich with flawed but likable
characters and...will be sure to delight readers and
have them sighing happily with that sweet ending."
—*Harlequin Junkie*

Scarlet Wilson won
the 2017 RoNA Rose Award for her book
Christmas in the Boss's Castle.

PROLOGUE

DARCY HELD HER hands in her lap, twisting one of the green leaves in her bouquet. 'Where is he?' she asked again, knowing that her voice sounded awkward with strain. She could see the sweat at her dad's collar.

The chauffeur gave a difficult smile. 'I'm sure it will just be a few minutes. Most brides aren't as organised as you and are usually running way behind. We're here dead on time. It's almost unheard of.'

He tugged at his jacket and Darcy looked down at the gold watch on her slim wrist. She could see the hint of pale green near the church's main doors. Her sisters. The bridesmaids had gone ahead as planned. But it seemed that they too had arrived before the groom.

Darcy took a deep breath. She was already worried about Laura. The pale green colour that had looked so beautiful in the early planning stages of the wedding had washed out her already paler than pale sister, making her look sicker than she wanted anyone to know she was.

It was a mild summer's day, but would Laura be cold? The bridesmaids' dresses were strapless, and Darcy didn't want her sister to have to hang around the church entrance—getting more chilled by the second—because Damian couldn't organise himself enough to get to his own wedding on time.

They'd often joked about how chaotic he was—the polar opposite to Darcy, who planned things to perfection. They drove each other to distraction, but opposites attracted, didn't they? That was what people always said, and Darcy assumed they must have been fated to meet.

A brisk breeze caught the jacket of the chauffeur and Darcy made up her mind. 'We're getting out,' she said to her father, who started in surprise. 'I'm not having Laura stand in the cold. We can all go inside and wait in the foyer. I'll get Fizz to call Damian and see where on earth he is. The other car has probably broken down or something.'

Her stomach gave an uncomfortable twist as she gathered up her skirts and opened the car door, stepping out onto the road outside the church. She waved her hand at the photographer, who tried to stop her as she strode up the path towards her sisters, her father hurrying behind her.

Her mother was sheltering in the foyer, her pale pink hat perfectly positioned on her head. 'What's going on?' she asked Darcy.

Darcy looked from side to side. The minister was hovering in the background, clearly as unnerved as the rest of them. The chauffeur appeared beside Darcy. 'Can you give my sister your jacket for a few minutes, please?' she asked.

He looked surprised, but after one glance at frail Laura he immediately nodded and slipped his jacket off, and around her shoulders.

Fizz—who had been missing for a few seconds—appeared from the side, a phone in her hand. 'Darcy—' she said in a croaky voice '—come here.'

Darcy's stomach plummeted. She knew. She knew what was about to happen. But she didn't actually believe it was about to happen to her.

Fizz had gone ahead with a few family items in the bridesmaids' car. Just normal things, like touch-up make-up, phones, emergency snacks and safety pins—because you never knew when you might need a safety pin. The overnight bags were already at the reception hotel.

But Fizz was currently holding a phone in her hand. It was silver. Which meant it was Darcy's. Fizz had the same phone in pink, and Laura in green.

Darcy handed her orange gerbera and dark green leaf bouquet to her mother and walked over to Fizz. She spoke in a low voice. 'What is it?'

Fizz looked pained. 'I heard your phone pinging. I think you have some texts.' She blinked, and Darcy knew her sister was blinking back tears on her behalf.

She calmly took her phone from her sister's hand.

The screen was still lit and the first few words of the message were clearly visible. I am so, so sorry.

Darcy licked her lips. Her throat was instantly dry and her skin prickled uncomfortably. She slid the message open with her finger then blinked at the length of the message. Damian had never been known to be long-winded. But it seemed today he'd made an exception.

Her eyes scanned the message as tears she didn't want to shed blurred her vision.

'I'll kill him,' came the voice of her father behind her, who had obviously read part of the message over her shoulder. 'I'll find him, and I'll kill him.'

And Darcy knew that in that second her father, the most placid man on the planet, meant every word. He adored his girls. She knew he would lay down his life for any one of them.

Every part of her body was shaking. But she was determined to be strong. She didn't want her family to see her break. Not after everything they'd been through together. The last few years with Laura's illness had taken its toll on every one of them. Her mother and father had aged visibly. They didn't need any more stress. Not when Laura was still at risk and only part way through her treatment.

Darcy lifted her head. This was her mess. No one else's. Her heart squeezed when she thought of all their family and friends currently sitting in the church, waiting for her and Damian.

A braver woman would walk in, tell them that he'd changed his mind and invite them all back to the hotel for a party—after all, it was already paid for. That was what other brides on social media did, wasn't it?

But even though Darcy knew her family and friends would put up a good front on her behalf, she knew that wasn't what she wanted. She wasn't that kind of person.

She took her phone and did a search. It took a few seconds to pull up a hotel that she'd looked at in the past but was always out of her price range. A few presses of some buttons and she'd booked herself in for the next five nights.

She kissed her sisters and her mum and dad on the cheeks. 'Thank you all. But you know that Damian isn't coming.' She shook her head, trying to pretend her voice wasn't trembling. 'I know I should go and tell people, but I just can't do it. I need some time to myself.' She tilted her chin up, feeling a little braver. 'I've booked a hotel. Please invite our guests back to the reception, some of them have travelled a distance. Look after them.'

'Darcy,' Fizz said, her arm immediately on Darcy's. 'I'll come with you. You're not going by yourself.'

Darcy pulled Fizz in tight. 'Look after Laura,' she whispered in her ear. 'Her next round of chemo is two days away. Look after her for both of us.' She pulled back now, not trying to hide the tears streaming down her face. 'We're the Bennetts. We'll get over this,' she said, the family motto they were all familiar with. 'I love you all,' she added before she gave a nod to the chauffeur. 'Will you take me where I want to go?'

The man gave an immediate nod and Darcy turned and started walking away from the church, not wanting to look back at her family.

She couldn't. Not now.

Not when her heart was breaking.

Not when she had no idea what might come next.

CHAPTER ONE

THE TWO SISTERS held hands as they sat down in front of the solicitor. His invitation to them had been like a bolt out of the blue. The date was seared on both of their hearts. It was the date that Laura had died. Today was the five-year anniversary.

Darcy felt as if a lump had settled directly in the centre of her chest. She was conscious of Felicity's hand in hers. Her fingers were cold. Had she lost weight? Darcy wasn't sure.

They'd spent the last few years living in different parts of the country, her in Edinburgh and Fizz in London. Where once all three of them had been in constant contact, since the loss of Laura, things had changed. There had been no fall-out, nothing dramatic. But the miles between them had enabled a distance to form in their relationship—almost as if they lived in separate bubbles. They still chatted on occasion, and texted, but their connection had changed—as if something was missing between them and they both felt it hard.

Fizz was usually effervescent, occasionally flighty, and jumped from one thing to the next. She had bags of energy, but today seemed a little more subdued. Maybe Darcy was overthinking things? It could be that Fizz was just as nervous as she was about being called to the solicitor's office.

'Ladies.' Darcy jerked at the deep voice. Mr Cochrane's slim frame filled the doorway. 'Thank you for coming.' He shot them a warm smile as he crossed the room and sat down behind the desk.

He was in his late sixties, with a neat grey beard and carefully trimmed hair. The last time Darcy had been here was when he'd spoken to the family about Laura's will. She'd still lived with their parents but had owned a car and had some savings and a few treasured possessions. They'd all been surprised she'd made a will, but had carried out all her wishes once her small estate had been settled. So why on earth had Mr Cochrane invited them back to his office today?

He gave them both a nod and opened a file on his desk. 'It's nice to see you both, and I am conscious of the date.' He paused and took a breath. 'But today's meeting was intentionally called on this date.'

Darcy glanced anxiously at Fizz, who seemed just as bewildered as she was.

Mr Cochrane clasped his hands. 'It's Laura that asked me to invite you both here today.'

'What?' said Fizz quickly, her brow furrowing.

Mr Cochrane held up his hand. 'She gave me some instructions, and it is those instructions that I'm following.' He glanced at them both, and Darcy could sense something.

'The truth is,' he continued, 'Laura was worried about how you would both cope once she was no longer here. She described the three of you as the Terrible Trio.' As soon as he said those words Darcy couldn't help but smile.

'She left some instructions that if in five years' time neither of you were settled with a partner or had a family, she wanted to leave something else for you both.'

He slid a paper across the desk towards them. Both of them instinctively reached out for it then gave a nervous laugh. 'Go on,' Darcy said to her sister, waiting as Fizz lifted the paper and held it in front of them.

Fizz started reading, her voice trembling. *'Time has passed and I hope both of you are happy and healthy. I'm not sure where you are in life right now, but if you're both here today it's because I've left you a final task to fulfil*

for me. Although Mr Cochrane handled my will and distributed my millions to the masses...'
Fizz's voice broke and she wiped a tear from her face. She gave a little laugh and turned to Darcy, who had the biggest lump in her throat. 'I can just hear her voice—hear her saying these words.'

Darcy nodded and brushed a tear from her own face. 'Me too.' She swallowed, even though the lump was still there, and took over the reading from Fizz. *'I kept a little something back. A policy that Mum and Dad had for me as a child, and has remained in the bank—on my instructions, under the care of Mr Cochrane. I wanted to keep this little pot of money for something special. My bucket list.'*

Darcy dropped the hand that was holding the paper. 'Her bucket list?'

It was an expression she hadn't heard in years.

Mr Cochrane gave a gentle smile. He nodded to her to continue reading.

Darcy took a breath and lifted the paper. *'I want you to take the money, split it between you and fulfil the items on my bucket list over the next month. I want to push you both to maybe do something you haven't. I want my sisters to have fun. Have fun in my memory.*

Know that I am right by your side when you do all these things. I love you girls, Laura.'

Darcy turned the paper over. There was no writing on the other side.

Fizz spoke first. 'Where's the bucket list?'

Mr Cochrane handed over two sealed envelopes, the names on the envelopes were in Laura's handwriting.

Now the tears did start to fall. Darcy reached out quickly and held it to her chest. Holding something that her sister had written for her a number of years ago tugged every emotion she had. She was glad she was sitting down right now because she wasn't sure if her legs would carry her.

After a few moments Fizz spoke. 'Why two envelopes? Are we doing the same things? Have we to do them together?'

Mr Cochrane held up both his hands. 'The instruction I was given is that you can both interpret your lists the way you think best—so I'm not entirely sure if they are identical or not. What I do know is that she wanted you to do these things your own way. So you've to do the bucket lists separately.' He raised one eyebrow. 'There was a mention you might need a companion or friend for some things.'

Darcy sat back in her chair and breathed out. This was the last thing she'd expected. A bucket list? She hadn't had one of those since she was a child—or a teenager at least.

He handed over a further item for each of them. Darcy blinked at the figure. 'This is the amount of each share of Laura's final gift to you both. If you give me current bank details the money can be transferred to your accounts.'

Fizz said the words out loud. 'It's more than I would have expected.'

Mr Cochrane gave a nod. 'Laura trusted me to invest it for the last few years on her, and your, behalf.' His smile was sincere. 'I think she would be happy with how things have worked out.'

They left the office in stunned silence, Darcy still clutching the envelope with the bucket list to her chest.

The connection to their sister was still there. It always would be. The Terrible Trio. Her heart ached at those words. Sometimes she'd wondered what nickname their father would have given them if there had only been two. The Dangerous Duo? Even the thought felt like betrayal.

She swallowed again. She'd never got over Laura's death. It always felt as if a part of them was missing. How could she go on and live a happy life when her sister had never got that chance? Those feelings of guilt had never left her, no matter how hard she tried to rationalise them. It was all just so unfair.

She glanced sideways at Fizz. They'd grown apart over the last few years. Not deliberately. But with Darcy living in Edinburgh, Fizz in London and both of them adults with their own life, it seemed inevitable, even if it did make her heart twist and turn.

She'd already lost one sister. And this event just gave her the harsh reminder that she couldn't take her other sister for granted.

'What do you want to do?' Fizz asked before Darcy had a chance to speak.

She glanced around her, unsure of what to do next. Both of them had to be feeling a bit strange—how could they not?

'Let's go for a coffee,' suggested Fizz.

'No.' Darcy shook her head in a way that was very unlike her. 'Let's go for a drink.'

Fizz blinked, and then followed Darcy as they walked down the road. It didn't take long to reach a fairly reasonable-looking hotel and they made their way to the bar.

'Something to toast our sister,' murmured Darcy as she scanned the bar.

'It's a cocktail,' said Fizz without a second's hesitation. 'It has to be.' She swiped the cocktail menu from the bar and scanned it as the bartender approached. 'Porn Star Martini,' she said.

They sat in comfortable silence as the bartender made the drinks. Darcy knew that her sister's brain was spinning just as much as hers was. But in some ways she and Fizz were very similar. Laura had been much more practical. She would have wanted to talk things through. But Fizz and Darcy both needed time to process things. To sort them out in their own time and in their own way.

As he slid the drinks towards them, Darcy picked hers up, knowing that they would drink them in entirely different ways. As predicted, Fizz downed her prosecco shot first, then held her glass with the mango cocktail. Darcy gave a small laugh and mixed her prosecco in with the cocktail—as Fizz shook her head—then lifted her glass to her sister's.

'To Laura. We loved her and miss her every day,' she said.

'To Laura,' Fizz agreed. 'And whatever she has in store for us with this bucket list.'

CHAPTER TWO

DARCY TURNED THE letter over and over in her hand. She was back home in Edinburgh, trying to make sense of what had just happened.

The aroma of the tea drifted towards her and she poured some from the teapot, cradling her cup in her hands as she looked out at the Scottish countryside.

For a bride who'd been stood up at the altar, things had actually turned out okay. The hotel she'd booked into in the city for five nights had given her a taste for Edinburgh. She'd been able to look at career opportunities that would allow her to rent a place on the outskirts. Her cybersecurity degree had led her from one job to another, with salary increases along the way, with much of her work being done remotely.

Her increase last year had allowed her to buy this cottage on the outskirts of Edinburgh, and although all the original features and stonework had been kept at the front of the cottage, the extension at the back had a glass wall that looked out onto the rolling green countryside and trickling stream nearby.

The farm next door had some fence gaps that allowed a chicken or sheep to occasionally appear in what was supposed to be her back garden. But Darcy didn't mind in the least.

She loved her peaceful countryside view, who needed a TV? She had neighbours close enough to not feel isolated, but far enough away to give her the space she desired.

Her life was settled. Her life was simple. Her life was quiet.

Which was why the bucket list from her sister was giving her so much trouble.

The four items listed for Darcy were:

Do something that scares you.
Grab a friend and have a mad twenty-four hours in a European city that you've always wanted to visit.
Make a lifelong commitment to something or someone.
Find somewhere peaceful—a space to share—to reflect on what you want out of life.

These were just the rough notes. Because alongside the typewritten page were scribbles in Laura's handwriting. Darcy was pretty sure that the notes Laura had written for her would be entirely different than the notes she wrote for Fizz.

Across the top of her page, in writing so familiar it made her heart ache, were the words:

You need to learn to connect with people again, Darcy.

She hated that her younger sister, five years ago, had known Darcy better than she knew herself.

Laura had never really been a fan of Darcy's fiancé Damian. Darcy had dated him for three years, and been engaged for one before their almost-wedding. They'd met at university—he'd been studying geography—and they had settled into a comfortable relationship. He'd struggled with Laura's illness. He'd never been nasty, but had sometimes clearly been frustrated when Darcy had cancelled plans at short notice because Laura was unwell.

At one time he'd accused Darcy of always prioritising Laura over him. She'd denied it at the time, but now, looking back, she could see that she clearly always had—and wasn't the least bit sorry about it.

The fallout from her never-to-be wedding

hadn't been extreme by any means. Darcy had taken herself to Edinburgh for five days, walked around the city, ate room service, joined a night-time ghost tour and spent an hour talking to a lonely elderly man in a café one day. Arthur had lost his wife of fifty years and was heartbroken. Darcy was the first person he'd spoken to all week.

She'd reached out and held his hand in hers, wary of his paper-thin skin. She'd told him about being left at the altar, and he'd decided it was his job to cheer her up. His strong accent had thrown her at first, but she'd concentrated, and her ear adjusted quickly. By the end of the hour, just having that short-term connection with someone had given her hope and she'd left with his phone number in her pocket and called him every week since.

She'd headed home, sold the house she'd bought with Damian and started looking for another job—one that meant she could get even further away. There had been no shouting or screaming. Damian had been level with her, telling her that even though they'd been in a relationship, she'd never really been 'there' and he didn't want to spend the rest of his life like that. The words hadn't stung at the time—she'd still been numb about being left at the altar. But in the years since she'd understood them a little better. He'd been right. She hadn't been invested the way she should have been. She hadn't been wildly in love. She'd been comfortable. She'd never pined for Damian after he'd ended things with her. Yes, she'd been sad, upset and unsettled. And everything about that event had bled into her present-day life. Whilst she'd dated over the last few years, she'd never found anyone that she'd wanted to go all in for. Something always held her back.

Darcy closed her eyes for a second, imagining Laura looking down on her and hearing her voice in her ear.

You've isolated yourself. You have to get back out there. What's happened between you and Fizz? Yes, you have a beautiful house, but what else do you have here?

Her computer gave a sharp buzz and she jerked, moving on automatic pilot to sit in her bright red ergonomic chair and click the button to take the video call. Libby's face flashed up on the screen and Darcy relaxed. Her friend from uni had moved to Australia a few years ago and was doing just as well as Darcy, except she had found a husband along the way and had a six-month-old baby.

'I've been thinking,' said Libby without pausing for a second to say hello.

Darcy couldn't help but smile and put her

head in her hands. 'It's always dangerous when you think, Lib.'

Libby laughed, her blonde hair partly covering her face. 'I've been thinking about the photo of the list you sent me.'

Darcy groaned. 'Now, I *know* this is dangerous. I should never have sent you it.'

'Rubbish.' Libby smiled, her thick Welsh accent still present. 'You had a moment of madness as you were getting on the plane to come back home, and thought you would share the list with your best friend on the other side of the world.'

She lifted a glass of wine to Darcy. 'You also knew I'd be sleeping and you'd be safe from a response for a while.' Her smile broadened.

'Oh, no,' said Darcy, her stomach clenching. 'I know that look.'

'I had a baby who was teething. I was up most of the night rocking her back and forward. And while I did that, I found a whole heap of things I thought you could sign up for.'

Darcy looked down at her cup of tea. 'I don't think this is going to be strong enough to get me through.'

'You know Edinburgh's a great city,' said Libby. 'There's lots going on. All you have to do is look.'

Darcy leaned her head on one hand and held

up the other. 'Okay, hit me with it, but just know, I'm not agreeing to anything until I've had a chance to think about it.'

'I want you to know I'm versatile,' continued Libby.

'Why do I have a feeling of impending doom?'

'Rubbish,' scoffed Libby. It really was her favourite word. 'I found things that you could use for either *"Do something that scares you"* or *"Make a lifetime commitment to someone or something".*'

Darcy had let her head slump back into her hands, but it shot up at this point. 'Tell me you didn't sign me up for something.'

Libby did her best to look innocent. 'So, hear me out. I found adult gymnastics—which could be scary, a church was looking for a Scout leader—that could come under a lifetime commitment.'

'I don't know a single thing about Scouts, don't you dare sign me up for that,' threatened Darcy.

But Libby wasn't planning on stopping going through her list. 'I also found pottery, painting, book clubs, curling, jogging, a netball team, a women's rugby club, but none of these seemed challenging enough.'

'How long was Charity up for last night? And why do you look so awake?'

Libby shook her head. 'I'm not really awake. I'm just in some kind of hazy, glazed state. Lack of sleep does things to your brain.' She held up one finger. 'But then I found something good.'

Now that Darcy looked closer, she could see a glint in Libby's eye. Libby had never done well with late night studying and lack of sleep, so she wasn't too sure she should argue with her.

'Do you remember years ago when we used to watch Saturday night TV as we were getting ready to go out?'

Darcy nodded slowly.

Libby tipped her head to the side and imitated Darcy's voice perfectly. 'And you always said there was *no way* you would do that.'

Her heart sank like a stone. There had been two Saturday night shows on rival TV channels. One involved intricate dancing, and one involved being on a stage and doing...something, as the judges buzzed contestants off for being... Libby's favourite word again—rubbish.

She couldn't quite find her voice right now. Either option made her feel sick.

Libby beamed. 'So, we know that Laura wanted you to go back out and meet people. What about this?'

The copied and pasted poster flashed up in the chat on her screen.

Carnival Ballroom Dancing
Variety Hall, Edinburgh
Every Monday at seven p.m.
Want to learn the quickstep? The samba?
The foxtrot? The Viennese waltz or the
paso doble?
Come along!
Bring a partner or we'll find one for you!

'No.' All of Darcy's automatic defence mechanisms kicked into place. 'Not a chance.'

'Oh, come on!' said Libby, an edge of humour and scorn in her voice. 'I could have picked a parachute jump, abseiling, or diving off the top of a mountain.' She leaned forward into the camera and put her hand on her chest. 'But remember, I know you. I was there when you shuddered as the celebs had to learn to dance with their professional partner, then some stomped around the dance floor and others flew like butterflies.'

'And you knew I was terrified of it.'

'Just like I know that you're equally terrified of heights and deep water. I picked the lesser of the evils.' Libby looked decidedly pleased with herself.

Darcy took a long, slow breath. She'd been

pondering the list for a few days and got nowhere. The truth was, she was scared to start.
Scared to take the steps that Laura was pushing her towards. She wondered if that was the
reason she'd actually shared the list with Libby.
Deep down, she'd known that Libby would
push her on.

'Okay,' she agreed, as something flashed
into her brain. Those words: *Bring a partner
or we'll find one for you!*

Arthur. Five years later, he was still in her
life. They had occasional lunches together,
or afternoon teas, or sometimes even met in
the Princes Street Gardens. The last thing she
wanted to do was be up close and personal with
someone she didn't know. Arthur was a gen-
tleman. Plus, he was eighty-five. They could
sit out the vigorous dances and maybe just try
the Viennese waltz. Would she be able to per-
suade him?

Something else pricked in her brain. She'd
heard that some of these kinds of classes were
full of older women. Maybe Arthur could meet
someone?

'This might not be a bad idea,' she said,
straightening up.

'Eureka!' declared Libby. 'So, will you sign
up?' Almost instantly a link appeared in the chat.

'Did you plan this?'

Libby shrugged. 'Told you. I've had some time on my hands.'

Darcy looked at her friend again. Libby was always immaculate. It didn't matter if it was the middle of the night for her, or if she'd only had a few hours' sleep. But did looking good mean anything?

'Are you okay?' she asked carefully.

'Yes, why?' Libby's brow furrowed.

'It's just…you've said you hardly had any sleep. But you still seem so…well, great.'

Libby gave a nod of understanding. 'Remember I have my mum, dad and Charlie to help too. They all look after me. I'm fine, honestly.' She tilted her head to one side. Libby had always been perceptive. 'What about Fizz? How was she? You haven't said much.'

'Not much to say. We went for a drink afterwards. But neither of us opened our letters together. It just felt too…personal. She texted me later and I know that we have roughly the same things to do—but Laura suspected we might interpret them differently.'

'So, any day now I'll hear about Fizz joining a nunnery or taking a vow of silence for a year? I can't imagine there's much in this life that scares your sister. At least none of the outrageous stuff that scares the rest of us.'

Darcy rested back in her chair and let her

shoulders finally relax. 'I think you'd be surprised. Fizz puts on a good face to the world, but she's not quite as brave as everyone thinks.'

Libby gave a slow nod and raised her glass. 'Well, I'm toasting you and your dancing. And I might send you a little surprise.'

'What kind of surprise?' Darcy was instantly suspicious. Libby could be wicked at times.

Libby winked. 'Guess you'll just need to wait and find out.'

CHAPTER THREE

ARTURO FABIANO WAS never nervous. He couldn't remember a single time in his life that he'd been nervous. Except now. And except here.

It was ridiculous. He walked past the unassuming entrance of the Variety Hall for the second time and shook his head.

He'd left things to the last possible second, hoping some kind of emergency might arise that would get him out of this. He glanced at the phone in his hand for the last time. *Ring!* But the phone stayed stubbornly unlit.

Giving his sister away at her wedding was an honour, of course it was, and after the death of their father, a few years before, he was delighted she had asked him. Delighted right up until someone had reminded him of the father of the bride dance he'd be expected to fill in for.

Dancing had never been an Arturo thing. While some of his friends had slid around the dance floor as teenagers, Arturo had charmed his way around the bar and the dance floor edges instead. For years people had complimented him on his looks, his business acumen and his family values. But no one had complimented his dancing skills, because he'd made it a rule not to embarrass himself.

Now? He stared at the panel outside the Variety Hall announcing the weekly activities held there. Now, it seemed like he was going to have to learn some kind of dancing in order to not let his sister down.

'Coming in?' asked a petite older woman with white hair. She had one of those intense gazes that gave the impression people didn't normally argue with her.

'Yes,' he said quickly, holding out his arm for her to go first, then striding up the steps as if he hadn't walked past them twice already.

He gulped as he entered the large hall filled with chattering voices. The scent caught the back of his throat. Perfume, soap, dancing shoes and in Edinburgh, of course, the smell of wet umbrellas and damp coats.

'You're new,' said another older woman, moving closer, along with a few of her friends.

Arturo gave a weak smile, wondering if they pounced on all new attendees. His eyes scanned the room. At the other side was an older man with a woman around Arturo's age. She had blonde hair in a ponytail and a puffy red skirt. She looked every bit as nervous as he did, and kept tugging at the edges of her skirt.

A woman with her hair in a bun and a black leotard with a floaty skirt over the top approached him. She walked with an elegance that suited her. 'Arturo?' she asked.

He nodded gratefully.

'Margaret.' She held her hand out towards him. The woman he'd emailed about the classes. She ran her eyes up and down his body. 'You strike me as someone who doesn't usually feel like a fish out of water.'

'You could say that,' he agreed, his tense shoulders finally relaxing a bit. Margaret could be anywhere between fifty and sixty, her dark hair had streaks of grey and she had the lean body of a woman who had danced all her life. As she glanced around the room at the hotchpotch of dance fans, he could see the patience on her face, and he sent a silent prayer upwards.

'Maybe this wasn't the best place for me to learn. Maybe I should have asked for private lessons.'

She side-eyed him. 'You're that bad?'

He laughed. 'I could be.'

She tapped his arm. 'Let's wait and see.

There are a number of newbies here tonight. Let's see how it goes.' Her smile was reassuring. 'I promise that I'll be able to teach you enough to glide your sister around the dance floor. You'll be fine.'

She walked away, her movements all long legs and graceful limbs. An hour. That was how long this class lasted. If he could get through this, he might have to take some time to rethink things. Thankfully, there was no one here he knew. His friends would be in hysterics if they knew he was taking dance classes.

And Arturo was determined to keep this quiet.

'This is a bad idea,' said Darcy to Arthur. 'I should never have asked you to come.'

Arthur straightened his shoulders as he looked around. Another woman nearby gave him a shy smile.

'Like flies around honey,' breathed Darcy. This might be a bad idea for her, but it didn't look like it was going to be a bad idea for Arthur. She could see the number of women in his age range who were already trying to catch his eye.

And she couldn't blame them. He was tall, trim, with a dapper beard and maroon waistcoat. Arthur knew how to dress.

'This might not be so bad,' he mused.

There was another guy at the opposite end of the room. He'd glanced in her direction a few times, and at first she'd wondered if he was one of the instructors. His dark hair and broad frame, as well as his impeccably fitted suit, would catch anyone's eye. But even though he looked like a man who turned heads, he didn't look like a dance instructor.

At least, he didn't seem to have the confidence she imagined went along with being a dance instructor. In fact, he looked every bit as uncomfortable as she was.

Margaret, the lady who'd greeted them when they'd first arrived, appeared in the middle of the room and clapped her hands above her head.

'Everyone. Get ready to start. We'll begin with some gentle warm-up exercises and stretches to get us all ready. Make sure you have some space around, and follow my lead.' She gave a nod to someone and some music started.

Gentle exercise. Darcy could manage that. She stared down at the red lightweight tulle skirt that had appeared in the post from her friend Libby. She hadn't even been sure she should wear it, but a quick text from her sister had encouraged her.

She followed the exercises, rolling shoulders, swinging arms, bending and stretching. It gave her a chance to look at the room around her. The Variety Hall in Edinburgh had been used for more than a hundred years. The wide, light wooden floor was deluged with sunshine that streamed through the central glass domed ceiling above them, with tiny insets of stained glass. It currently gave the illusion that it was a beautiful and bright day outside, whereas the wind tunnel known as Princes Street gave an entirely different version of the day.

The warm-up exercises finished quickly, and Darcy found herself face to face with Arthur, following some very simple steps. It was clear that at some point in his life he'd done this before and was a complete natural.

As she glanced around the room it was also clear that many of the participants had been coming for a while. Hardly anyone seemed as confused as she was.

'Move around!' said Margaret, clapping her hands above her head, and Darcy's eyes widened as she realised that everyone else was swapping partners. She'd only planned on dancing with Arthur, but he was swept away from her eagerly by another woman, and she found herself in the arms of an older grey-haired woman.

'Barbara,' she sighed quickly. 'I always end up as the man.'

Darcy couldn't help but laugh. She started to relax a little. The people around her were lovely. Some took things very seriously, but most were there to keep fit and have fun. A few were reliving dancing from their youth. All were patient with Darcy if she messed up a few steps. She kept her eye on Arthur and he seemed to be having the time of his life.

Her heart ached, remembering how lonely he'd been when she'd first met him. Since she'd moved to Edinburgh they'd become firm friends, but now she wondered if she should have tried some more sociable activities with him earlier.

Darcy twirled around and side-stepped straight into her next partner. His large frame filled her vision in the expensive cut of an Italian suit and a whiff of entirely masculine and woody noted aftershave. She caught her breath and looked up, just as he stepped on her foot.

'Yeow!' she said, hopping and catching her foot in her hand. The soft leather shoes she'd been recommended for class certainly couldn't deal with the weight of his muscular build.

'I am so sorry,' he said immediately, but her ear didn't take in the words. Her ear took in the accent. The rich Italian accent that fitted entirely with the dark handsome man in front of her.

For a second, she wondered if this was all some elaborate game show. Libby and Fizz had concocted this whole thing together as a kind of 'gotcha'. The guy was actually some actor and was probably supposed to make this whole thing a nightmare, to see how much it would take her to flip.

She pushed the thought away almost as soon as it formed. That was the trouble with having an active imagination. It could take her down dangerous paths and ridiculous scenarios. Anyway, no one could really top being stood up at the altar, so what would be the point?

The man's hand was on her arm, his other trying to reach her foot as she hopped around. Heads had turned and were watching them.

She put her slightly squashed foot back on the ground and tried not to grimace. 'It's okay,' she said automatically. 'It will be fine.'

Fine *after* she'd raided her bathroom cupboard for some painkillers and probably sat it up on her sofa for the rest of the night.

His face was marred by a deeply furrowed brow and he spoke some rapid Italian that she didn't have a single chance of following. His words were musical, the language rich and smooth. It did things to her skin. Things she didn't recognise at first. Not until the skin prickles made their way directly to her spine.

The jolt was instant. Disturbing. And then strangely awakening.

It was a long time since she'd felt any kind of attraction to a man. It wasn't as if she'd lived like a monk—or, more appropriately, a nun, for the last five years. But everything had been very casual for her. She hadn't really allowed herself to be invested in anyone since Damian. Losing both her sister, and Damian in such a short space of time had made her wary of risking her heart again. It was so much easier to keep a protective barrier wrapped around herself and focus on other things. Like work or the renovations to the cottage. Both of which had been ultimately time-consuming.

Someone squeezed her hand gently and she jolted back to reality. It was him, of course it was him, and now he was looking at her with concern.

'Arturo,' he said softly, as if he'd already said it before. 'I am Arturo Fabiano. I am so sorry.'

She blinked. 'Darcy Bennett,' she replied, meeting his dark brown eyes.

He shook his head in disgust. 'I should never have come here. It was a stupid idea. How on earth can anyone learn to dance in a few weeks? I should have known better.'

Her interest was instantly piqued. 'You want to learn to dance in a few weeks? Why?'

He took a breath and sighed. She could tell by the expression on his face this meant something to him. 'My sister is getting married. Our father died a few years ago, and she's asked me to give her away.'

Something tugged at Darcy's heartstrings. Words could be simple but she understood the heartache behind them.

'I'm sorry about your dad.'

She watched him swallow, clearly surprised she hadn't just kept talking. He paused and met her gaze. For a moment they didn't move, held in place. *'Grazie,'* he said in a low voice.

The people around them had started moving again, and it was clear they were blocking the flow. Arturo looked around them and held out his arms automatically—one on her shoulder, one at her waist, for them to get back into the rhythm of those around them.

As she slid her hand into his, the warmth of his palm seemed intensely personal. As she tried to remember the steps that Margaret continued to shout out loud, Darcy took a deep breath. 'So, I take it giving your sister away also means doing one of the dances at the wedding?'

His expression was almost a grimace and

she had to hide the smile that threatened to dart across her face.

'Yes,' came the short reply.

The furrow had appeared on his brow again and she could tell he was concentrating on the steps they were doing. Every now and then he glanced down, obviously trying not to step on her toes again.

'Is this your first time here?'

'Yes.'

'Mine too.'

Now, his eyes came up from the floor and locked gazes with her again.

'Why did you come?'

Her stomach twisted a bit. Arturo might be tall, dark and handsome, but he was also a complete stranger. She wasn't sure she wanted to share about Laura and the bucket list. A Variety Hall filled with a hundred other people just didn't seem like the place for that conversation. 'I have an older friend—Arthur.' She nodded in his direction. 'I persuaded him to come because I'm trying to get him out more.'

It wasn't the truth, but it also wasn't completely a lie. Her brain made a few more connections and she prayed he wouldn't ask how she and Arthur had met. Telling him the humiliating being left at the altar story was even less appealing than the personal bucket list story.

Arturo followed her line of sight. 'That sounds nice.' He gave a smile—the first one she'd seen from him. It had an easiness about it and changed his expression completely. His furrowed brow could be intimidating. But the smile? Well, that could make knees weak on the other side of the room. 'He certainly looks as if he's going down a storm.'

Darcy nodded. 'And I couldn't be happier for him. This looks like it's giving him the boost he needs and deserves.'

Arturo gave her a curious glance but she didn't fill in any of the blanks. Instead, she looked straight into those brown eyes with a renewed burst of confidence. 'So, Arturo Fabiano. What do you do for a living?'

He raised his eyebrows. 'Just call me Indiana Jones.'

She couldn't help but smile. 'You're an archaeologist?'

He shook his head as they took another few steps. 'I find hidden treasures.'

Now it was Darcy's turn to raise her eyebrows. 'What does that mean?' She wasn't quite getting the steps right, but at this point she didn't care. 'Don't archaeologists spend all their time digging in the dirt?'

'I've done that,' he agreed with a nod. 'I've worked on sites at Pompeii, Egypt, Turkey and the UK. Now, I do mainly retrieval. Mostly it's art—paintings, sculpture, artefacts.'

'So, who do you work for?'

There was a fleeting expression. Was that embarrassment? 'I work for one of the Italian national agencies.'

She felt a little tremor down her spine. It was the way he said the words. Was he like an art kind of James Bond? 'I get the impression you're not looking for new works—or new artists.'

He gave the smallest dip of his head. 'Let's call it a recovery operation.'

Darcy was intrigued. She'd heard of people trying to retrieve pieces of art that had been stolen during wartime. Was that what he did?

'How do you do that? And how do you know what to look for?'

He spun her around and she almost lost her footing because she was no longer paying attention to the instructions but more to the man holding her in his arms. 'Sorry,' he laughed.

She shook her head as a woman tapped her arm. 'It's time to move partners again.' She glanced pointedly at Arturo.

Darcy tried not to laugh and went to step back, but Arturo shook his head. 'Maybe it's best to leave us out of the swapping. We're both complete beginners and we don't want to spoil anyone else's dance experience tonight.'

He said it so smoothly but commandingly that the woman blinked, gave a half-annoyed look and moved away.

He leaned forward and she caught his woody aftershave again. 'Hope you're not offended. But I don't plan on being picked apart by all the experts here tonight. Plus, I don't want to stand on anyone else's toes.'

'Whereas mine are already flat?' she countered.

She could see the waver in his eyes—trying to tell if she was joking or not—but his face broke into a wide smile again. 'Exactly,' he agreed.

'So, you've interrogated me,' he said good-naturedly. 'What do you do?'

'Cybersecurity.'

'You're a hacker?' His eyes widened and it was Darcy's turn to laugh.

'Sometimes. It depends what the job is. I've worked with banks to improve their security systems. I've worked with private companies who've purposely asked me to hack into their systems in order to find any points of failure. Sometimes I'm just giving general security safety advice or training for staff.' She'd actually done a whole lot more than that but, thanks to contractual obligations, wasn't allowed to say.

'You must be a woman of many secrets.' He was teasing, but the comment hit a nerve, immediately causing her to tense. This attractive man was a perfect stranger. She really knew nothing about him. And she wasn't quite sure she was ready to admit the strange pull she felt towards him.

She was so out of practice with all this. In a flash of panic, her eyes darted to his hand, checking to see if he wore a wedding ring. Thankfully, his finger was bare. Relief. In years gone by, she would have always checked before continuing a conversation with a stranger, particularly one who seemed to be flirting with her.

As the music stopped, she dropped her hands from his. 'I should check on Arthur,' she said quickly. 'See if he needs rescuing.'

Was that disappointment on his face? 'Of course,' he said graciously. 'Thank you,' he added.

'For what?' she asked as she stepped back.

'For making an evening I was dreading...' he paused and gave a hint of a smile '...not quite as bad as I thought.'

She could swear an army of butterflies just fluttered next to her skin. Darcy just smiled and headed across the dance floor towards Arthur. He gave her a knowing look as he glanced in Arturo's direction.

'Darcy, my dear,' he said with a twinkle in his eye, 'I think we need to talk.'

CHAPTER FOUR

ARTURO SPOKE IN rapid Italian to his counterpart. He'd been chasing this stolen artefact for years. It had belonged to a fellow Italian family over a hundred years ago and had been stolen in a midnight raid on their property. There had been no trace of the painting for years—meaning it had likely been stolen to order by another family. Now? He'd heard rumours of house clearances and basement sales, along with a few whispers amongst the antique dealers. He pulled up his screen and noted the next flight to Catania. With another few words, he completed the call and leaned back in his chair, looking out over the city.

Most people were surprised that he'd temporarily based himself in Edinburgh. Arturo had travelled the world with his job and stayed in many cities. But after an initial visit a few years ago he'd liked the charm and vibe of the ancient city. Some of the streets seemed to brim with history, and there were a surprising number of experts relevant to his field nearby. A flight to London was only an hour away and nowhere was ultimately out of his reach. Plus, after the death of his fiancée, followed a few years later by the death of his father, Italy had too many memories and reminders. Arturo had realised quickly that he needed a little space and some different scenery in order to move on with his life.

But had he moved on? Not really. Two big losses had made the usually steady ground shake beneath his feet. He wasn't even sure he was ready to. But at least in Edinburgh he was away from the microscopic glances of his family, their love, their opinions and their strong-armed influence. And the truth was, Edinburgh already held a little space in his heart.

His fingers moved quickly, booking his flights and accommodation. He could have asked his assistant to do all this for him, but he'd already sent her a piece of research work this morning and would rather she continue with that. He glanced at the return flight. He would be back in time for the next dance class.

His fingers froze on the keypad and he leaned back, staring out of his glass-walled office towards Edinburgh Castle. The thought had just slipped into his head, like a little seed secretly sown. Arturo's skin prickled. He couldn't deny that the woman he'd met the other night had piqued his curiosity. He was sure there was much more to Darcy Bennett than met the eye. He liked that.

It had been so long since a woman had sparked his interest. His American fiancée had held a role similar to his. They'd met first on a dig in Egypt, then again when they were both trying to retrieve the same piece. It had seemed like fate. The whirlwind engagement had surprised both their families. And even though Faye and himself could be like ships passing in the night, the spark hadn't died. At least not until she had.

She'd been in Japan at the time, at Shibuya, the world's busiest crossing. An investigation had shown images of Faye being distracted by her phone and not paying attention to a speeding car. Arturo had spent hours wondering if it had been he that had distracted her. She hadn't answered the phone, but pulled it from her pocket to see who was calling. If she would have answered or not, no one would ever find out, because things had happened in a flash.

He'd checked times around the world and was sure he'd been in a meeting at the time, but it had always stuck in the back of his head.

Who had called Faye and distracted her at the very second she needed to be paying attention to the world around her?

That hadn't been part of the investigation because no one had cared. It was irrelevant. But thoughts about it still occasionally found a space in his dreams.

His family had encouraged him to date again, and he was sure at some point he would. He'd taken a few female friends to dinner, but he hadn't considered them dates because he'd had no romantic intentions.

The woman he'd met the other night—Darcy?—had thrown him. At first it was her fellow awkwardness. Then, when she'd spoken, he'd realised she was English instead of Scottish. He'd grown so adept at listening to the Scottish accent these days, another accent had thrown him for a second. He hadn't expected to look into a pair of blue eyes and feel a pool of warmth inside him. It had almost been like flicking a switch back on.

He was relieved that someone else with no experience had attended the class. When he'd realised just how pretty and intriguing she was it had sparked his interest. Arturo had spent a long time focused on work. It was all-encompassing, particularly when his team knew they were close to revealing some hidden secrets and finding a long-lost painting or artefact. Occasionally, his job was dangerous. People paid millions to own some of the pieces he'd come across, and not all had been originally sourced by legal means.

But his job was also a family legacy. His father had trained him, alongside his two degrees in Archaeology and Art History. Even as a child, he could remember tense moments when his father had clearly been threatened because of pieces he was pursuing. Arturo was almost sure threats had been made towards his family too.

It was part of the reason he struggled to connect. Attraction to women was never a problem, but connection…was an entirely different story. If he knew his job could potentially put someone at risk it would be fundamentally wrong to pursue anything other than a short-term fling. At least that was what he always told himself.

The thought had played in his mind around Faye's death. She'd had a similar job to him. But, to the best of his knowledge, Faye had never encountered any real threats. And there had been no connection between the driver that had hit her and any work she had been pursuing. Her death had been nothing but a tragic accident. But still the thought remained.

The fact that his personal family fortune

meant that neither he nor his father had a real need to pursue the careers that they had didn't really feature in his thought processes. Both of them loved the job that they did. And Arturo couldn't see himself ever leaving this role.

But it made meeting a woman tricky. There had been the odd occasion in his life when he'd been targeted by a woman whose purpose was to entice details around his latest research. It had even come into his head at the first meeting with Faye. But Arturo had quickly learned to recognise those people. Darcy Bennett? An English girl, working in cybersecurity and dancing with an older man in the Edinburgh Variety Hall—on the exact same night that he attended—would be a feat that even a psychic couldn't have planned.

So he felt comfortable about thoughts of Darcy. Particularly when he remembered her little quirks. She'd been just as nervous as he was. She had a habit of biting her bottom lip or curling a piece of hair around her finger. She'd tugged at her bright red skirt a few times as if she'd had second thoughts about wearing it.

But there were also the things that she couldn't hide beneath her façade. The way she'd glanced over at her older friend on a regular basis, to make sure he was surviving. The fact she had no problem looking Arturo right in the eye and responding to his questions. She hadn't even pretended for a second that she was a good dancer, which gave him the sense that Darcy was straight down the line—honest, true and had a sense of humour. This was a woman he would be happy to see again.

Maybe this time he could ask her out for a drink? It might be a bit forward but, if he made it to the class in time next week, who knew what could happen?

His phone buzzed and all his thoughts went back to work. Darcy Bennett and her red skirt would have to wait.

CHAPTER FIVE

'BE COOL,' Darcy said out loud as she walked alongside Arthur, then wondered if she were saying it for him or for herself.

It was official. Arthur had a date after the dance class tonight. It was already prearranged at a nearby quiet bar with Connie, a woman he'd been texting since last week.

He was nervous. Arthur hadn't dated anyone since his wife had died, and said he didn't even remember what to do.

'Be yourself,' Darcy had reassured him. 'She's already met you and likes you. That's a great start.'

She glanced along the street, wondering if she might catch a glimpse of her tall, dark Italian. She'd had major regrets since last week, wishing she hadn't made an excuse to get away, and had instead continued the conversation with him.

Libby and Fizz had both been in touch about

the dance class and she hadn't even mentioned him. She didn't want to be interrogated on someone she might never see again.

'Ready?' asked Arthur, tilting his elbow towards her. She slid her arm through his and they climbed the stairs.

The class was busy again, people were stripping off coats and outdoor shoes. Margaret was making a few introductions, then moved to the centre of the room.

'We're splitting into two groups this week. Anyone who wishes to try the quickstep and some swing, go on through to the Callaghan Hall next door. Anyone who wishes to continue with the Viennese waltz, we'll start with that in here, then move onto the foxtrot.' She clapped her hands above her head. 'Find a partner for the Viennese waltz if you are staying, and you'll be staying with that partner for the first half of the class to concentrate on frame and footwork.'

Arthur gave a nervous cough and Darcy gave him a nudge. 'Go on, go and find her.'

He'd barely taken a few steps when there was a tap on her shoulder. 'I'm looking for a partner for the Viennese waltz, are you taken?'

The accented words sent an unexpected tremor down her spine and by the time she spun around she knew she had a stupid grin on her face.

She put her hands on her hips and tried to be much cooler than she actually felt. 'You came back?'

'For a second round of torture. I'm actually going to come on Wednesday too. I need to up the ante here to get myself ready for this wedding.'

'You're deadly serious?' She was secretly impressed.

He raised his eyebrows. 'You haven't met my sister. If I step on *her* toes the way I stepped on yours…' He let his voice trail off but he was still smiling.

It was the easiest thing in the world to put her hands into his and join him on the dance floor. Margaret came around and sternly positioned them. 'Hips straight, head up, shoulders back, chest out.' The words were like commands, and she could see from Arturo's face he was trying hard not to laugh.

'We'd better concentrate,' she whispered.

His eyes stayed on Margaret as he leaned forward and whispered in her ear. 'I'll concentrate better if you agree to come for a drink with me afterwards.'

For a second, her mouth was instantly dry. The thing that had circled her dreams most nights this week was actually happening. She licked her lips. 'Well, it just so happens that Arthur has a date after class, so I am free.'

Arturo grinned. 'He does?' His head inclined to watch Arthur and his new female friend and she could tell his interest was genuine. 'That's great.'

She nodded and Arturo studied her for a few moments. 'I'm scared to ask, but do you want to go to the same place that they are? Just in case you're worried,' he added swiftly.

'What if I told you they were going to bingo?' she teased.

'I'd tell you that I missed that skill set in Italy. You'll need to show me the ropes.'

She laughed. 'You're safe, they're going to a pub. It might not be your scene either though.'

He shrugged easily. 'You've said yes. I don't care where we go.'

There was something about those words. While her stomach gave a little flip, she actually felt relaxed around him. Yes, they barely knew each other. But in this day and age he acknowledged the fact she might want to be around friends rather than alone with a relative stranger. It was considerate.

Margaret's voice cut through her thoughts. 'Music is starting now, get ready.'

They both straightened up, concentrating

hard. One hour later, her back stiff from trying to keep both her posture straight and lean back the way she should, Darcy's legs were aching.

'I think I've got the natural turn and the reverse turn, but that's about it,' she admitted.'

He gave her an appreciative smile. 'That's two of the basic steps. We're doing good.'

'Why did your sister pick the Viennese waltz? Why not the normal waltz? You could probably have got away with just shuffling around the floor for that one.'

He nodded. 'I probably could. But she likes to be specific, and she's planned her wedding to perfection. She did offer to find someone to train me.'

'She did? From Italy? Wow.'

'Yip, she sent a list of instructors and was slightly annoyed when I told her I would find my own.'

Darcy somehow knew that 'slightly annoyed' was likely a toned-down term.

Arturo glanced across the room. 'Do you want to stay for the foxtrot?'

She laughed. 'You are joking, aren't you? Buy me a drink, please. Let me just tell Arthur that we're leaving.'

She moved around the edges of the dance floor and gave Arthur a kiss on the cheek. 'Good luck,' she whispered.

'You too,' he said in a low voice, while keeping his arms around his current dance partner.

Darcy collected her coat and walked out into the autumn evening with Arturo. Edinburgh could frequently see four seasons in one day, but the air was warm this evening, with the sun setting behind the castle in a brilliant array of oranges and purple. She stopped for a second and took a deep breath.

Arturo paused at her shoulder and looked in the same direction she was. 'Stunning, isn't it? My office has a view of the castle and the sunrises and sunsets are the best thing about it.'

She gave a deep sigh of appreciation before turning to him. 'And in those words you've just told me that you spend entirely too much time in your office.'

He nodded in agreement. 'You're right, I do. But sometimes it's worth it.'

She gave him a curious look. Just how much was there to find out about Arturo Fabiano?

He glanced along the street. 'How about a drink somewhere special? I know a place that does lovely Italian wine.'

She raised her eyebrows. 'It had better be public.'

He laughed and nodded. 'Don't worry, it is.'

A few minutes later he took her into the best known and most expensive hotel in Edinburgh.

She didn't even want to know what the prices were in the bar here.

But once they'd settled in comfortable leather chairs and there had been a few smiles towards her dance skirt, Arturo leaned forward. 'Do you have a preference between white and red?'

'If I was sophisticated, I'd say red. But the truth is I like white. Red always gives me a headache.'

He lifted his finger then shook his head, laughing at himself. 'I am saying nothing.' He ran his eye down the wine list and motioned to the waiter, who returned with a bottle of white wine.

He signalled he didn't need to test the wine, and watched as the waiter poured it into the glasses. She hadn't even taken a sip before the waiter returned with some bread, olives, oils and a bowl of nuts.

'Do you think we look hungry?' she whispered.

'Maybe,' he replied with a smile.

She sipped the wine and gave a sigh. 'Lovely.'

'I'm glad you approve.'

Darcy relaxed back in the chair, looking at the comfortable surroundings. There was a quiet ambience in the bar, with a number of the tables taken and low-voiced conversations taking place around them. 'This place is nice,' she said.

He pressed his lips together for a moment. 'What?'

He pulled a face. 'I should probably tell you that technically I've been staying here for the last few months.'

'Here?' She couldn't help but be astounded. People stayed here for one night, maybe two at a push. But months? What would be the price tag for that?

'Seemed like a central location.'

She took another sip of her wine. 'I guess you could call it that.' She narrowed her gaze towards him. 'I am not coming upstairs to your room.'

He held up a hand. 'And I didn't intend to ask—no, that might not have come out the way it should. I just thought I should tell you now, in case it came up later and you were annoyed I hadn't mentioned it.'

He looked genuinely worried and she decided to let him off easy.

'It's fine. Now I know why you knew there were good Italian wines here.'

He nodded through towards another room. 'There's sometimes a harpist playing in the gallery above in the room next door. It really is a nice place.'

She knew it was a really nice place. Most people who stayed in Edinburgh did—it just wasn't an everyday place, and that made her a little nervous. It wasn't as if money was a big thing for her. She made a better than average salary on her own, the private sector paid handsomely for people with her cybersecurity skills. Her cottage was her pride and joy, and she had some savings in the bank and was already paying into a pension. But she was beginning to suspect that Arturo was in an entirely different league when it came to money.

She raised her glass to him. 'So, tell me more about your sister's wedding. You said she was a planner.'

He smiled. 'Cara was born a planner, and I think in truth she's actually been planning her wedding since she was around six years old.'

'When is it?'

'In a few weeks. I don't have much time to perfect my dancing skills. That's why I said I would go to the extra class this week.' He gave her a thoughtful look. 'Are you a glutton for punishment—will you join me?'

Darcy gave a small gulp, a little taken aback by his straightforwardness. 'I'll need to think about it,' she stalled. 'Tell me more about your family.'

He paused for a moment, watching her carefully with his dark brown eyes before taking a sip of his wine and talking again. 'I only have one sister, and her fiancé is a man from another part of Italy who she met at university.'

'Do you like him?'

He gave a careful smile. 'It takes a special man to stand up to my sister.'

Darcy wrinkled her nose. 'What does that mean?'

'It means that I think he's up for the job. She's been very precise about her wedding details and he has on occasion told her no, and to be reasonable.'

She was amused at how wide his smile was. 'And you can't say no to her?'

He laughed and shook his head, 'Oh, I've spent a lifetime saying no to my sister, with varying degrees of success.' He waggled his hand in the air. 'But things are different now.' His voice quietened. 'Her dream was for our father to walk her down the aisle. That can't happen now. So I feel as if I have to give her some—what do you call it—leeway?'

Darcy nodded. He took another sip of wine then leaned forward, eating up the space between them. 'So, tell me truthfully, Ms Cybersecurity, why are you really at a dance class? You like it as much as I do,' he joked. 'And it can't all be about Arthur.'

She took a breath, not sure how truthful to be. 'It is partly about Arthur.' And she did genuinely mean that. She just wished she'd thought about something like this a few years ago. 'He's really come out of his shell. If you'd seen him when I first met him five years ago, he was very different.'

'But he was still grieving then, wasn't he?'

The words settled over her like a comfortable hug. It was the combination of things. The way he said the words, the tone and the understanding. She knew he'd experienced the grief of losing his father a few years ago, and it was clear he comprehended what that did to a person.

'He was,' she said simply then leaned forward too. There were now only inches between their faces, but what she needed to say wasn't something she really talked about in public, or at all. She needed this space to feel private, as if it were just theirs. She said the words before the courage left her.

'The reason I'm at the class is because my sister left me a bucket list that she wanted me to complete. She died five years ago, and I was only given it last week. I'm doing it in her honour.'

She spoke so quickly that she was sure all the words ran together. Would Arturo even have picked them all up? His English was excellent, but Italian was his first language.

His eyes widened by the slightest margin, but she was close enough to see it. Was this too close?

He reached out and put his hand over hers. 'I am so sorry about your sister.'

There was silence for a few moments, and Arturo didn't try to fill it. His expression was sincere. He seemed to know that those few words would be enough.

Darcy sucked in a deep breath and just let it sit. Experience had taught her that if another human being had experienced grief then they seemed better at acknowledging it and understanding it in others. That seemed to be true this evening.

The warmth from his palm flooded up her arm. He couldn't possibly know how much this all overwhelmed her. Attraction. It had been a long time since she'd felt it. But attraction along with connection? She couldn't remember feeling like this in for ever.

Her past relationship with Damian was now a distant memory. He was married to someone else and had a family of his own. She strongly suspected he might have met his wife before Darcy and he had actually split. But suspicions and repercussions were not a path she'd ever wanted to go down. Once a relationship was over, it was over. She didn't dwell. She didn't dissect. At least that was what she told herself because, deep down, the hurt was still there.

But as she felt warmth radiate up her arm she was asking herself a whole host of other things. While she'd dated and had a few casual relationships, she knew she'd built walls around herself.

It was her duty to protect herself from hurt. Being stood up at the altar, closely followed by the death of her beloved sister, meant she'd learned to shield herself from the outside world. Edinburgh, and her home, had become her protective sanctuary. Was she lonely sometimes? Of course she was. But being a bit lonely was nothing compared to having your heart ripped out.

She woke up to a beautiful view every morning. The flexibility of her job allowed her to live her life more or less as she pleased. All of a sudden, though, she was questioning if that was enough. If that was what she wanted. And the hot contact from Arturo's palm was doing strange things to her body.

He lifted one eyebrow. Did he know? Did he know the wave of panic that had just enveloped her? Or was this something else entirely?

That lifted eyebrow was enough distraction to

centre herself again. He gave an amused smile. 'A bucket list? Hers, or yours?'

Okay, a normal question. She could handle that. Thank goodness he couldn't see all the places that her mind had just gone. Darcy leaned back, disconnecting their hands, and rested her elbow on the table, letting her head sit in her hand.

'Mine, I guess. But I had no say in it, and she wrote it.' She bit her lip and added, 'I should have said I have another sister—Felicity. Laura wrote a bucket list for us both.'

'Wow,' said Arturo, sitting back in his chair too and lifting his glass of wine again. He picked up the wine bottle from the bucket next to them and topped up their glasses. 'I'm settling in for the ride.'

She smiled. He was making this easy on her. And, for the first time in for ever, it felt nice to share.

'Okay, so are your bucket lists the same?'

Darcy pulled a face. 'So, I don't really know.'

'What do you mean?'

'We were together when we were given them, but we didn't open them together.' She sighed and admitted out loud what she'd been holding in her head. 'In a way, I'm glad we didn't. Because mine has little handwritten notes from our sister Laura, and that just made it way more special. I imagine Fizz's is the same.'

'You call your sister Fizz?'

'Yes, it's like a nickname. You have them in Italy, right?'

He gave a slow nod. 'Yes.'

'So, Felicity's is Fizz. She couldn't say Felicity as a child, so she called herself Fizz. It stuck. As for the bucket list, she likely has the same kind of notes that I have. And we were also told we could interpret the list of things any way we wanted.'

Arturo's brow furrowed. 'This is just getting curiouser and curiouser.'

She smiled at the common phrase.

'So she told you to go to a dance class?'

'Not exactly. She told me to…' Darcy paused for a second as she tried to remember the exact wording '…"Do something that scares you".'

Before Arturo had a chance to laugh, she waved her hand, 'Oh, I know, I know, it's not exactly as scary as a parachute jump, or diving with sharks, but—'

'No, wait,' Arturo said quickly, holding up his hand. 'I am right there with you. Dancing is scary. Particularly if you didn't spend your youth—' he smiled and she could see him trying to recall something '—the lady that cleans the offices calls it "jigging around the dance floor".' He gave a little shuffle of his shoulders as he said those words, and Darcy burst out laughing. Several heads turned and she put her hand up to her mouth.

'Sorry,' she whispered. 'But you tried a Scottish accent there and it was perfect.'

'Really? I'll tell Doris, she'll be impressed.'

'Was it her that told you about the dance classes?'

He nodded. 'She heard my sister on a video call to me. Told me she could find me a dance class instead of my sister.'

He tapped the side of his nose. 'And, let me tell you, I've done a parachute jump and I've dived in a shark cage. Those things have nothing on being in that dance hall, all eyes on you, and your feet, back, arms and body all doing entirely separate things.'

She lifted her free hand. 'See? You get it. You understand. I've never been a natural dancer. I never like all eyes on me.' She gave an awkward kind of shiver. 'And I don't really like getting that up close and personal with people I don't know.'

He blinked, his face deadpan. 'So if Margaret had suggested the rumba?'

She lifted her glass to him. 'I would have broken the four-minute mile getting out of that place.'

Arturo leaned forward and clinked his glass off hers. 'To us,' he agreed.

They smiled at each other, and that flip-flop sensation was in her stomach again. This guy was doing strange things to her. This didn't feel like the previous flirtations she'd had. This was just...different.

'So, why do you think your sister is telling—presumably both of you—to do something that scares you?'

Darcy's skin chilled a bit and she set her wine glass down and started pulling a few pieces off the bread. 'Our family changed when Laura was sick.' It suddenly occurred to her that Arturo hadn't asked what happened. 'Her death wasn't an accident. She had acute lymphoblastic leukaemia and had a variety of treatments over a number of years. Other things happened too.' She paused because she wasn't ready to go there yet. 'So there was a lot of strain on our family.' She gave a sad smile. 'Fizz and I are actually twins. Laura came along a few years later but we were all inseparable. My dad used to call me and my sisters the Terrible Trio. We actually all got on. We had our own friends and things, but there's nothing like having sisters.' She pressed her lips together for a second, deliberately not letting herself get lost in memories. 'Once one of us wasn't there any more, things just changed. Fizz is in London now, and I'm in Edinburgh. We don't see each other as much as we should.'

As she said the words out loud, she realised how true they were. She knew that right now her eyes were shining with unshed tears. 'I think Laura probably knew what would happen. She was kind of the linchpin—the steadying force. She knew we would probably retreat into ourselves. I guess her bucket list is to try and push us out there again.'

She sat back and took a breath, trying to sort things out in her head. It was as if she'd already known all that but saying it out loud made the difference.

Arturo was looking at her curiously. 'You have a twin?'

She nodded.

'Identical?'

Darcy shook her head. 'No. We do look like sisters, but we're not identical.'

Arturo gave her a few moments. 'A bucket list is an interesting idea. What else does she have on it for you?'

Darcy took a handful of nuts. 'Another three things. I haven't quite worked out what I'll do for them yet. One of them is to grab a friend and have a mad twenty-four hours in a European city somewhere.'

'That's a good one.' He reached over for some of the bread. 'What's your favourite city then? Barcelona? Vienna? Paris? Madrid?'

She shook her head. 'I've been to a few. But I'm toying with somewhere I've never been before.'

'You have a list?'

'In my head.' She tapped the side of her forehead. 'Pisa—do I want to stand and do the traditional tourist picture with my hand outstretched?'

She demonstrated and he shook his head. 'Oh, please, no.'

'Or Venice? I know that they're hideously expensive, but I might want to try a trip on a gondola and look at St Mark's Square.'

He gave a slow nod. 'Venice is a cool place, particularly at night.'

She raised an eyebrow. 'Not sure if I should ask questions about that or not.'

He gave her a smooth smile and she breathed in, trying to not let her body respond to just how unconsciously attractive Arturo Fabiano was. It wasn't just her. She'd seen the occasional glance from other females in the bar area. They probably wondered what Arturo was doing with her, sitting here in Edinburgh's poshest hotel with her silly dance skirt on.

'I considered Milan too, and Rome. I'd love to see the Colosseum.'

'Once seen, never forgotten,' he agreed. Then he looked up. 'All your cities are in Italy. Is that just a coincidence?'

Her cheeks started to flush. 'Well, yes and no. It's a place I've never been. I did have plans to go there a few years ago and…' she looked out of the large window to the street outside '…I ended up here instead.'

'Edinburgh instead of Italy?'

She swallowed and spoke as lightly as she could. 'Don't ask. And I have looked at other places. But some of them I've been to—Paris and Euro Disney, Berlin, Crete and mainland Spain on traditional girl holidays or city breaks. My father took us to Switzerland and Denmark on family holidays years ago. But Italy—' she looked upwards '—it just slipped through my grasp.' She tilted her head and connected with those eyes again. 'Which part of Italy are you from?'

'Verona,' he said without hesitation. 'The city of love. *Romeo and Juliet* land.'

She put her hand on her heart. 'Oops, sorry I didn't mention it on my wish list.'

'You're forgiven,' he said. 'If the *Romeo and Juliet* play didn't exist, we probably could have kept Verona as Italy's hidden secret.' He held up both hands. 'Unfortunately…'

'Is that where your sister's wedding is?'

He nodded.

'In a hotel in the city?'

He took a few seconds to answer, stroking his wine glass between his fingertips in a way that instantly dried her throat. 'Actually, she's getting married in our estate.'

'What?' The word came out before she could help it. But of course. A man staying at the most expensive hotel in Edinburgh, with a glass office that faced the castle and wore suits like he did? Of course they'd have an estate. Not your average house in a normal street. She was kind of feeling stupid right now for not even considering this before.

Arturo spoke carefully. 'We have an estate in the outskirts of Verona. My family have lived there for generations. The house is big enough to hold the wedding, and Cara has always wanted to get married in our home.'

He gave a soft laugh. 'I doubt I'll recognise the place by the time I get home. I can only imagine what she's been up to in my absence.'

'Are you worried?'

He gave the slightest shake of his head. 'Cara has impeccable taste. She won't have done anything long-lasting.' He pulled a face. 'At least I hope she won't.'

Darcy was still trying to get over the fact that Arturo had an estate. That, plus the good looks and the Indiana Jones-style job. She felt as if she could be in her own version of a film.

'How do you like the wine?' He leaned over and topped up her glass again.

'It's lovely,' she admitted, 'but no more for me. I'm a lightweight.'

'Will you join me at the next class?'

She lifted her glass. 'Ah, you've been bribing me.'

'Not at all. I just prefer learning with someone who is at the same stage as me. You know why I'm there and why it's important to me, so...'

Something rushed into her head. Darcy had never been impetuous, and even the second she had the thought, something told her she should check with either Libby or her sister before she proceeded any further. She took a slow breath, trying to calm her heart-rate that had instantly speeded up. Could she really ask him to join her on a mad twenty-four-hour tour? It was certainly playing on her mind right now.

She swallowed the last of her wine and looked Arturo Fabiano in the eye. When was the last time she'd taken a chance? When was the last time she'd done something spontaneous?

'I'll come on Wednesday with you, if you agree to have a mad twenty-four hours with me in an Italian city of my choosing.' She waved her hand. 'I'm paying, of course.'

He blinked. For a moment he just sat there, and part of her cringed, a tiny part started to die inside.

Her mouth automatically started talking again. 'Who better to show me around than a real-life Italian who can show me the best bits, and help me with the language?'

Silence, but only for a second.

Something flickered in his vision, then he blinked again and raised the rest of his wine towards her. 'It's a deal. But I'll warn you…'

His words dangled in the air. She was still getting over the 'deal' word and trying not to punch the air.

'You'll warn me what?' Her voice had a teasing tone that even she didn't recognise. This was what good Italian wine and a surge in confidence did for her.

'Once we've done your mad twenty-four hours, I might ask you for something in return.' His eyes were fixed on hers. He had a teasing look in them too. 'Only if you agree, of course.'

Her stomach twisted and she wasn't sure how she would explain this turn of events to anyone else.

'I do a favour for you, and you do a favour for me,' he said slowly, in a smooth tone that made her feel as if dragonflies had just fluttered against her skin.

This was convenience, certainly for her, and it looked like it would be for him too.

She lifted a few of the nuts into her palm. 'I guess we'll just need to see what the future holds then.' She smiled back, nodding in agreement, and told herself she must be out of her mind.

CHAPTER SIX

FOUR DAYS LATER, Arturo pulled up outside the cottage and gave a low whistle. When Darcy had told him that she lived 'somewhere out in the sticks' he hadn't expected a white stone cottage set against a splash of green hills. It looked more like a painting than a real home.

He also tried to take a steadying breath. His family home back in Verona was more than a hundred times bigger than this. He had to be careful not to say or do anything to overwhelm her. Particularly when he knew what he was going to ask her in return.

Darcy Bennett was intriguing. He'd done a little digging. Some people might say that was off. But Arturo was used to doing a little digging on any new person he came across. With his line of work, and his family wealth, it paid to know who you were making friends with. Darcy Bennett was exactly who she said she was. She had a good job, and was well regarded in her field. When she'd given him her address for the pick-up to the airport, council planning records showed that she'd done extensive renovations on her cottage over the last few years.

The bright red door flew open and she stood there with a smile. Her blonde hair was pulled up in a ponytail, she was wearing black three-quarter-length trousers, flat shoes and a white shirt tied at the waist. 'Come in,' she shouted as she disappeared back inside.

He got out of his car, locked it—even though he hadn't seen another person—and walked to her doorway. A small bag was sitting just inside the door and he ducked his head as he stepped inside the cottage.

The whole place was much brighter and airier than he'd expected. To his left was a pale blue fitted kitchen with a large Aga stove that was popular in farmhouses. Through another door that was slightly ajar he could see a modern white bathroom. But the place that drew his attention was just ahead. As he stepped into what must be Darcy's sitting room, he saw a wall of glass that faced straight out onto the Scottish landscape. It was completely hidden from the road, out of sight from anyone else. The view was magnificent, and there was even a sheep wandering around outside, which seemed utterly uninterested in the new person through the glass.

It was six in the morning, and the sun was up with a little mist on the hills.

Arturo couldn't help but smile as he moved over and sat down on the cheerful multicoloured large sofa. Darcy was inside a cupboard, wrestling with some coats. She pulled out two. 'What do you think? Black or red?' She held them both up but he just laughed and held out his hands towards the glass wall.

'I think this place is amazing.'

'You do?' He could tell by the expression on her face that she was pleased. She obviously took pride in her home.

'Of course,' he said and nodded outside. 'You even have your own sheep.'

She laughed, 'Oh, that's Betty, and she isn't mine. She's the farmer's next door. There's a small gap in his fence that he keeps meaning to fix and she likes to wander through.' She held up the coats again. 'Which one?'

He stood up and walked over, touching one and then the other. The black one was made of wool, the red one a lightweight raincoat. 'Are you absolutely sure you want to take a coat?'

She looked surprised. 'Of course.'

'Italy's a lot warmer than Scotland.' He smiled at her.

She shrugged. 'I know. But I can't go away for twenty-four hours without a coat.'

'In that case, definitely the red. The black one will be too warm for Italy right now.'

She beamed. 'Where's a handy Italian when I need one?' She hung the black coat back in her cupboard and put the red one over her arm. 'Want to know what city I chose?'

She hadn't told him where they were going, and he didn't want to break it to her that it wasn't hard to work out when they were flying from Edinburgh Airport, but he played along.

She held up the tickets. 'Rome! It had to be the Colosseum. I've even bought us tickets.' She waggled them at him. 'I hope you slept well last night—the rules are no sleep for the next twenty-four hours.'

'I think I can manage that.' He smiled, wondering what on earth he'd got himself into. Through his family and his work, he had connections in Rome that he could pull at short notice. He could have got them into anywhere she might have wanted to go. But Darcy didn't need to know that.

They took one last look at the view and headed to the airport. Arturo's normal domain was the first-class lounge, but Darcy had insisted that she was paying for things since it was her bucket list, so he contented himself with buying them some drinks from the bar.

The three-hour flight was over quickly, and because they had no luggage they exited the airport swiftly.

'Where to first?'

She pulled a face. 'I want to see the Trevi Fountain, the Colosseum and St Peter's Square and the Sistine Chapel at the Vatican. What will be the busiest?'

He glanced at his watch and lifted his hand to hail a taxi. 'We'll go to the Trevi Fountain, then stop and grab some lunch. The Colosseum and Vatican always have queues—even when you have fast-track tickets. It is too hot to queue right now. So, let's start the way we mean to continue.'

The taxi ride was chaotic. Darcy sat with her face pressed up against the window and Arturo pointed out some of the other parts of Rome they might not have time to visit.

The streets around the fountain were packed with tourists, just like Arturo knew they would be. As they exited the taxi, he slipped Darcy's hand into his. 'Stay close,' he whispered as he threaded through the crowds.

It was warm already and by the time they reached the junction where the fountain sat it was wall to wall people.

'Is it always like this?'

He nodded, keeping threading through the throng of people. 'It can be like this at six in the morning, and in the middle of the night.' Arturo scanned the surroundings and found a spot where they could stand that was a bit quieter.

He pulled her in next to him and let her stand for a few moments taking in the giant display. 'A large part of this was hidden for a few years while the renovations took place. People still came, but now they are gone, a lot of tourists are keen to come back.'

'It's beautiful,' Darcy breathed, her eyes fixed on the white baroque fountain with its central figure.

'It is,' he agreed, watching the water flow through the fountain. 'Do you want to know some facts about it?'

She looked up at him, her blue eyes shining. 'Go for it.'

'So, *trevi* means three. It dates back to Roman times when there was an ancient aqueduct called the Aqua Virgo that provided water to the Roman baths and fountains of central Rome. It was built at the end point of an aqueduct at the junction of three roads. This construction finished in 1762.'

'That long,' she sighed. 'And look how popular it still is.' She leaned against him and he wondered if she was already hot in the Italian sun. For him the weather was mild, but the UK was always colder than Italy, and Scotland even more so.

He held out a hand towards it. 'Even though it's white now, it's been black and red before.'

'No way!' Darcy looked genuinely surprised.

He gave an amused smile. 'Not for any period of time. It was turned off and draped in black when an Italian actor died who starred in the most famous film made here. The red, unfortunately, was vandals, but it was cleaned up quickly enough.'

'Vandals? Here?' She shook her head. 'It just seems so ridiculous.'

He nodded. 'The fountain uses a massive amount of water—and you wouldn't want to drink from it. But thankfully, the water is recycled, so there's minimum wastage.'

'But what about the coins?'

They were watching as lots of people stood in front of the fountain and tossed coins over their shoulders.

'Collected every night,' he answered promptly, 'and they all go to charity. It's a crime to steal coins from the fountain.'

'Has anyone tried?'

'Oh, yes, and been caught. The most famous by a hidden camera.'

He gave her a nudge. 'Want to be a tourist and throw a coin in?'

'Of course.' She smiled and they edged their way through the crowd. Thankfully, most people posed for a photo, threw their coin and moved on. As she readied herself in front of the fountain, she smiled up at him.

For a second, his heart stopped. He hadn't doubted his attraction to Darcy had been growing, even though part of him told him she was wrong for him. Arturo moved around the world. Darcy seemed very settled in Edinburgh. He had a large, opinionated Italian family. Darcy seemed quieter. He wasn't quite sure how she would fare against his headstrong sister or occasionally outspoken mother. He wasn't sure they would ever be a good fit, particularly with the type of job he did.

And all these thoughts made him a little uneasy. Where had they come from? He still didn't know that much about Darcy—nor she about him. She'd told him her bucket list, and he'd told her about his father. But he knew that wasn't all he should tell her. Not if he liked her, and not if he thought this could go somewhere.

His phone pinged and he looked at the text. It was an Italian antique dealer who always had his ear to the ground. He wanted Arturo to get in touch. He was based in Rome, his shop near the Colosseum. Arturo contemplated for a few moments. He'd promised these twenty-four hours to Darcy. Would it be fair to go along?

He switched to his camera and held up his phone. 'Know that the legend says if you throw a coin in the fountain, it guarantees a return trip to Rome.'

'I think I can live with that.' She grinned, holding up her coin before tossing it over her shoulder and closing her eyes for a few seconds, her lips moving silently.

'What was that?' he asked.

'A secret,' she replied with a smile.

He grabbed her hand again and led her down one of the long nearby streets. Tables from a variety of restaurants lined the length of the street, and Arturo picked one that he knew did particularly good pizza.

'Can I order for you?' he asked.

She nodded as she sagged into the chair opposite and let her hair down for a few moments. At least here they were in the shade and the waiter brought them water, before taking Arturo's order.

Forty-five minutes later, Darcy was clearly revived after pizza, wine and some water. Her hair was back in a ponytail and she launched into her plan of attack for the Colosseum. The fast-track tickets meant they wouldn't need to queue in the sun and could start on one of the audio tours as soon as they got in there. It would still be warm. Unless Rome was surprised by showers, she wouldn't be wearing her jacket at all today. He waved his hand and settled the bill before she could argue, then took her to a nearby street to find a taxi again.

He heard it. The moment that she caught sight of the Colosseum and sucked in her breath at the marvel of it.

People could look at pictures online, but no one really understood the scale, size and beauty of the structure until they could actually see it.

Something about her reaction struck him deep inside. He was proud of his nation and its history. There was a real sense of delight that she thought the Colosseum just as fascinating as he did. What he would give to wave a magic wand and go back in time to see it in a past life. Once an archaeologist, always an archaeologist.

She tapped his arm. 'What are you smiling about?'

'Just wishing I had powers and we could go back and see this in gladiator times.'

'We can watch the movie,' she said with a face so straight he wasn't entirely sure she was joking. But then she threw back her head and laughed. 'I should have taken a photo. Your face was an absolute picture then.'

She started to climb out of the taxi. 'Please tell me you're not going to give me a list of all the historical inaccuracies in the film, and all the archaeological facts they got wrong.'

'Only if you really annoy me,' he quipped good-humouredly as he paid the driver and climbed out of the taxi too.

They joined the fast queue, waiting around fifteen minutes for entry, the supply of their audio tour and a book with the history of the Colosseum. Arrows showed where they should start, but Darcy was distracted.

She left the headphones dangling around her neck in her haste to climb some floors and get the full feel of the structure.

It was busy but, because of its size, there was plenty of space to find a spot of their own. Arturo couldn't help but watch those around him. He pointed over at a tour group of school-children.

'I was brought here with my school friends when I was seven. All of us just wanted to pretend to be gladiators and be down in the central arena.'

'Were you allowed?' asked Darcy as she stared down, then she frowned at him. 'But there's no central floor, it's all the dungeons underneath.'

'I know that…' He sighed. 'But we had over-active imaginations and wanted to pretend that the central floor was still there.'

Darcy just stood admiring the structure around her. 'How on earth did they build this more than two thousand years ago? The perfect arches. The symmetry? The details.' She kept glancing around as the tourists milled about, stopping to take pictures and admire different viewpoints.

'Want to go down to where the gladiators were held?'

She gave him a strange look, then shuddered. 'No. I can feel it.' She held out her hands. 'There's an atmosphere here. A…something. As soon as you walk through, it's as if a thousand souls are speaking to you.' She touched the stone. 'Every part of this has been here all this time. Even the colour. The grey, the pink, the flecks of white. What kind of stone did you say this was?'

'Travertine limestone, along with tuff—volcanic rock—and brick-faced concrete.'

'Even that feels of something,' she breathed as she continued to look around in wonder. 'Can you imagine the noise if sixty-five thousand people were in here? I really wish you had that magic wand.'

He nodded and they stood for a few more moments in silence. There really was no need to fill in the space. The Colosseum told its own story, and he could see how much Darcy appreciated. There were other people in here, videoing themselves and taking a photo of every step. But apart from a snap outside, Darcy hadn't got her phone out yet. She was just 'feeling' the place, and he liked that about her.

It was something that he'd always done at archaeological sites. Some people just couldn't wait to start digging or exploring in their enthusiasm to find something mind-blowing. But Arturo, and Faye, had liked to get the feel of a place. To sense the history, and the people who had gone before.

He had a flash of guilt for thinking of Faye when he was with Darcy. The truth was, Faye had faded from his thoughts with time. She would always be there. Particularly if he was doing something work-related that might remind him of past digs or conversations. But she'd moved from being a central figure to a pleasant memory. Was this why he'd started to feel the spark with Darcy? Was he ready to move on and think about someone else?

Darcy turned around, pulling his attention

back to the moment, leaning back and looking upwards. 'Imagine being in the cheap seats,' she said with a smile.

Arturo looked up too. 'What? You don't imagine you would have been in the special boxes with the Emperor and Vestal Virgins?' He liked that she was so enthralled by the place she was imagining it back in the day.

She laughed out loud. 'And where would you have been? Would you have been a senator?'

'I hope so,' he said, then screwed up his face. 'But maybe not. If I'd been a former gladiator, I would have been banned.'

'So you would,' she agreed as she flicked through the pages of her book. 'You, and the gravediggers.'

They both laughed out loud, then she sighed at the raincoat over her arm. 'Give me that,' he said, smiling. It was hot, and her skin was turning a little pink. 'I think you need some more sunscreen.'

'Really?' She rummaged in her bag. 'I'm wearing factor fifty. I just burn at the drop of a hat.' She rubbed some more sunscreen into her face, neck and arms, then handed it to him. 'You too,' she ordered, not giving him a chance to argue.

When he handed it back, she finally pulled out her camera. But before she even took a photograph she turned to him, her eyes squinting in the sun. 'Thank you.'

'For what?'

'For agreeing to come. For being able to speak Italian and keep control of the taxis.' She took a deep breath. 'For saying you would do this with me. I know I kind of pushed you into it. I know this likely wasn't your first choice— a mad twenty-four hours in Rome.'

He gave a little bow of his head. He knew her words were sincere. 'It's my pleasure.' And he meant it. Because it had been a long time since he hadn't focused entirely on work or family matters. Arturo couldn't remember the last time he'd taken a holiday. And even though this was officially only twenty-four hours, he was grateful for even that. He raised his eyebrows just a touch. 'You don't know yet how you're going to repay me.'

'Nothing dubious, I hope,' she replied quickly.

'Not at all,' he responded. 'Just know that I will likely need at least twenty-four hours of your time too.'

She frowned then smiled. 'Oh, go on then. Don't be all mysterious about it. Spill.'

He threw back his head and laughed. 'I will, on the way home.'

She shot him a mock angry face as she started to snap some pictures.

He hadn't realised how much he'd needed this until he was actually here. He took her phone and took some photos for her. 'Let's go for a coffee, and do you mind if we get out of the sun for a bit?'

'Not at all.' She finished smiling for the photos, then took her camera back and turned it to face them both. 'Smile,' she ordered, snapping them with the inside of the Colosseum behind them.

Without pausing, Arturo took his phone out too, taking an identical photo. He did it without thinking, knowing that he wanted to capture them both too. It suddenly seemed important to him.

'Can I pick the place for dinner tonight too?'

'Okay,' she said without a moment's hesitation.

They left the Colosseum, taking a few more pictures, then moving on to a café and sitting for a while drinking coffee, water, and eating cake.

'What time is the visit for the Sistine Chapel?'

She checked her phone. 'Five-thirty.'

'We have plenty of time. Do you mind if I visit a nearby antique store?'

Darcy looked momentarily surprised. 'Not at all. I'd love to look in an antique store.'

They finished at the coffee shop and Arturo took her hand again and led her down the streets until they reached a narrow alley with uneven stones. There was a variety of shops on the street, and Darcy looked in a few windows as they made their way down towards the green-canopied antique store.

Part of him wished he hadn't even mentioned this. It could be that Matteo only wanted a two-minute chat, but something in the pit of his stomach told him that it was so much more.

He pushed open the door and the bell sounded. Both of them blinked. The shop was much darker than the natural light outside and it took their sight a few seconds to adjust. A deep breath would let anyone know they'd just come into an antique shop. There was an odour of mustiness about the place but it wasn't unpleasant.

Darcy immediately made her way over to a glass cabinet to look at some jewellery.

A slightly rotund figure with spectacles perched on his nose emerged from the back of the shop. 'Arturo!' He couldn't hide the shock in his husky voice, and even Darcy started.

Arturo started speaking in rapid Italian in a low voice. 'You said you needed to talk.'

'Yes, but I didn't mean in person. I didn't think you were in Italy, let alone Rome.'

'Well, by coincidence I am. What is it you need to talk about?'

Matteo glanced over at Darcy. 'Who is she?'

'A friend. And don't worry, she can't speak Italian.'

'You're sure?' Matteo's glance was suspicious.

'Of course I'm sure,' snapped Arturo. He didn't even want Matteo to look in Darcy's direction.

'Come with me.' There was a flick of his head and a few moments later Matteo was showing him pictures he'd received of an artefact that Arturo, and his father before him, had been seeking for many years. It had been stolen from an old Italian count in New York eighty years before.

The beautiful painted sculpture was only the size of his hand, but the coloured paint on it looked as if it had only been done yesterday, even though it was apparently four hundred years old. Much of the artist's other work had been lost throughout the ages.

'Is it genuine?'

Matteo stared at him through his horn-rimmed spectacles. 'That's for you to say, not me.'

Arturo stayed silent, focusing on the pictures. 'Arrange a meeting,' he said, before glancing behind him to the shop. 'Let me know when. I have other business today.'

Matteo followed Arturo back out to the main

shop. Darcy smiled when she saw them and nodded to Matteo. 'Would I be able to see this, please?'

Arturo was surprised, he hadn't expected her to be interested in anything in Matteo's shop. Matteo immediately moved into his charming proprietor routine, which Arturo had witnessed on many occasions. He pulled his key chain from his pocket, unlocked the glass cabinet and pulled out the item she was referring to with obvious pleasure.

He switched to English easily. 'Oh, yes. An ancient late Roman gold garnet ring. The flat band is made from a thick hammered sheet of high carat gold and the garnet cabochon is set in the centre in a closed back setting.'

He held out the yellow gold ring with its surprisingly bright red stone. It had a slightly orange tinge to it and the stone was set in the middle of the ring. 'The gold is twenty-two carat,' he added as Darcy slipped the stone on her finger.

The gold wasn't finished in the way that any jewellery made in the last few hundred years was. The rough working was clear. And it was small, though Darcy could slip it on her right-hand ring finger.

She held up her finger, obviously caught by

the history. 'This is genuine?' she asked. 'And verified?'

Arturo tried his best not to smile. Matteo could occasionally be a charlatan in other respects, but with his antiques he was always above board.

'Of course,' Matteo blustered, a little offended.

'Can I see the paperwork?' she asked.

'It's in Italian,' he said dismissively as he walked over to a large cabinet.

'Luckily enough,' said Darcy astutely, 'I brought my own interpreter with me.'

Matteo shot Arturo a glance, fumbling through some files and producing the paperwork to verify the gold, setting and provenance of the ring. He gave Darcy a nod.

'I love it,' she announced. 'I'll take it.'

Arturo wasn't sure whether to be surprised or not. The price tag was a few thousand pounds. It wasn't that he thought Darcy couldn't afford it. He was more taken aback by the impulsiveness of her purchase. She handed over her credit card to Matteo, which Arturo quickly substituted for his own. She didn't notice, and shook her head when Matteo offered to package up the ring for her. She only took the receipt and a small box, which she put in her handbag.

Arturo exchanged a few more words with

Matteo about the potential meeting before they walked back out into the now blistering sunshine. Darcy was still admiring her ring. 'I feel as if I have a part of the day now,' she said simply, then put her other hand on her heart. 'Something to always remember my sister by, and keep the memories of my visit to Rome alive.'

Arturo was instantly a little wounded by the words. Wouldn't their ongoing friendship—or whatever it was—keep the memories alive?

But he could see by her face this wasn't about him. This was about her sister, and honouring her memory. He was wise enough not to say anything until Darcy turned to face him with a bright smile, holding her hand out towards him. 'Sistine Chapel?'

Then he slid his hand into hers and headed to hail a cab.

He wasn't quite sure what he would tell anyone about this day. His sister, although caught up in the last few whirlwind weeks before her wedding, would ask him a million questions in the way only a sister could.

In a strange way his heart ached a little that he couldn't have this conversation with his father. He'd been the wisest man that Arturo knew. Although he'd never interfered in his son's relationships, he'd been astute and full of good advice when it came to women. He wondered what his father would have thought of this Englishwoman.

Arturo knew that his mother had long expected him to marry an Italian woman, preferably from one of their peer group. She had been decidedly unhappy about his engagement to Faye. His father hadn't had the same expectations and had always told Arturo to follow his heart. He'd liked Faye and always been gracious to her. But—and it still made Arturo smile—he'd never given the follow your heart advice in front of his mother.

Darcy spun around as the taxi slowed beside them, almost tripping as both hands landed on his chest. 'Oops.' She smiled, the amber scent of her perfume assaulting his senses. She looked up, her pale blue eyes shining, energy emitting from every pore. Her happiness was infectious. 'This is the best day,' she said simply, staying still for a few seconds right under his nose.

The palms of her hands seemed electric through the fabric of his shirt. He wanted to stay there. He knew they were in a rush to reach the Sistine Chapel in time. But for the first time in as long as he could ever remember, Arturo Fabiano wanted to freeze-frame his life—capture this moment in time and keep it.

It had been so long since he'd felt like that. And he couldn't actually remember a time like that for him and Faye.

But Darcy? She was an entirely new person and all of a sudden he wanted to explore more, to push a little and see what might happen.

He knew that he would eventually let her know he'd been engaged before. But he still had a feeling Darcy had walls in place. It wasn't quite so apparent today. Today in Rome seemed to be a 'throw caution to the wind' kind of day. But back in Edinburgh she occasionally opened her mouth to say something, then clearly rethought and stopped.

He couldn't imagine what it might be, but one thing was for sure—he wanted to find out.

CHAPTER SEVEN

DARCY WAS FEELING as though she'd been swept off her feet. She wasn't sure how else to put it. It didn't matter that she'd actually swept herself off her feet by planning this whole twenty-four hours. She was consciously aware that while Rome was beautiful and fascinating, the same words could also be used to describe her companion.

Was now the time to mention meeting a handsome Italian to Libby and Fizz? She bit her bottom lip and quickly sent them the selfie of them both that Arturo had taken with her phone. As the taxi darted through the Rome streets, she typed two words: Loving Rome.

She tried not to look at herself too hard in the photo. One glance and she could see the glow coming from her, and exactly how happy she looked. She was sure her sister and friend would notice too. No doubt they would ask questions.

Her fingers twisted her new ring. There was

something wondrous about owning a piece that had history and had belonged to generations of women before her. The price hadn't fazed her, but she had found Arturo's colleague a little… shifty? Was that the right word? It seemed irrelevant now as they sped through the city towards the almost final destination of the day.

As they pulled up outside the Vatican entrance to the Sistine Chapel, the queue was still present. They climbed out of the taxi and Arturo guided her towards the entrance, where they showed their tickets.

'Do you know the way?' she asked Arturo, and he nodded and led them down a central corridor.

The walk to the chapel was long. History was all around them. If she'd been in Rome longer, she would have loved to spend a day on a whole Vatican tour, seeing the gardens, admiring all the tapestries and portraits and beautiful sculptures. As it was, she saw them all at breakneck speed since they knew the time of the last admission to the Sistine Chapel and she didn't want to miss it while admiring other parts of the museum. The inside of St Peter's Basilica would need to remain on her wish list.

As she walked along, Arturo by her side, interested in everything they were seeing and commenting on it all, it suddenly struck her that she might have been in a very different position.

At this point in her life, she could have been married to Damian for five years. And what struck her the most about that was just how much he would have hated this mad twenty-four-hour rush around Rome. He wouldn't have found enjoyment in this—in fact, he probably wouldn't have agreed to come. Museums, monuments and national buildings had never featured in Damian's plans. He just wasn't that kind of guy. She'd always known that while being stood up at the altar had been ultimately cruel, it had been the best thing for both of them.

The handsome man beside her was intelligent, gracious and the perfect companion. And the more hours she spent in his company, the more she realised it.

It was odd. Because she'd initially felt quite reserved around Arturo. But the more she got to know him, the more confident she became in being herself around him. He still didn't know everything about her—or she him—but gradually she could feel her walls and barriers beginning to come down.

It had been a moment of pure madness to invite him to join her. Some might infer she'd done it for convenience, and in a way she had.

But that didn't stop the little hiccups she had inside her body when he smiled at her, or their skin came into contact. There was nothing convenient about that.

There were still moments to pause and admire some of the artefacts. By the time they reached the entrance to the Sistine Chapel she was dizzy with the beauty around her.

There was a sign telling visitors not to take pictures and not to talk in the chapel. Even though they were part of the last group to enter, the chapel was still busy. It seemed as if everyone in the world wanted to see the same place that she did.

Arturo spoke in low Italian to one of the security guards at the entrance, who murmured a few words to him. As soon as they stepped inside Darcy was struck first by the heat, and then by how thin the air seemed.

But all that disappeared as she lifted her head to stare at the ceiling and the frescoes on the walls. She could hear whispers all around her, but was reluctant to join in. She wanted to be respectful of her environment, and take everything in.

Her first surprise was how bright the colours were on the ceiling and, as she moved closer to the wall frescos, just how much detail was actually included. The clothing, the hairs, the skin wrinkles were all presented in a way that made her want to reach out and touch it. Of course she didn't. The security presence in the chapel was heavy, but she could understand people being overwhelmed by the sight in here.

The second thing that surprised her was how small the chapel was. In her head, she'd pictured it as much bigger, but now she was here she realised she could cross from the entrance to the exit in around forty steps. Not that she wanted to. But she could sense people around her being hurried along.

Arturo put his hand at her back and gently steered her to one side, out of the flow of traffic. It gave her a few moments to take some time and look properly. From her childhood in Sunday school in her home town of Bath, she recognised several of the biblical scenes, such as the creation of the sun and moon, Adam and Eve, the garden of Eden and the Last Judgement on the wall behind the altar, its brilliant blue tones standing out brightly to her.

Eventually, a guard signalled it was time to leave and they exited at the side of St Peter's Basilica, by the entrance to the stairs to the dome.

Although the air in Rome was still warm, the gentle breeze was a welcome relief from the stifling crush in the chapel.

'Too many people,' she sighed. 'I don't know why I expected anything else from Rome's most favourite tourist attraction.' She leaned back against the nearby wall, letting the cool stone penetrate through her white shirt. Her hair felt sticky and she really wanted to sit down again.

She couldn't help but stare up at the steps of the Basilica and wonder if she should try to cram that in too. Her stomach gave a loud rumble and she laughed and put her hand over her abdomen.

'How about a choice?' said Arturo good-naturedly.

'What do you mean?' She took a deep breath, trying to clear out her lungs.

He waved his hand towards the street down from St Peter's Square. 'We could do dinner at one of the restaurants that face the Basilica and admire the view here or...' He paused for a moment. 'Or I know another restaurant that looks across to the Colosseum. What would you prefer?'

The breeze was dancing across her skin and finally cooling her down now. 'How about a drink at one of the street places that look up to the Basilica, and then on to the restaurant near the Colosseum?' She grinned. 'And just so we're clear, I'm looking for a cocktail right now.'

He laughed and they walked amiably across

St Peter's Square, stopping to take some photographs, and taking a few for some other tourists.

They stopped at a bar, drank some Rossinis then some Negronis and took some photos of the sun setting behind the gleaming white Basilica, before catching a taxi to the restaurant that Arturo had reserved for them.

Their table was on a rooftop terrace and, as they sat, lines of orange and violet were streaming behind the Colosseum. Their waiter took some photographs as Arturo ordered for them.

Darcy took the opportunity to drink some water as they waited for their food. 'I can't believe I've just had the chance to see the sun setting behind two of the most beautiful buildings in the world.' She held up her hands. 'It feels like magic.'

'Magic? Really?' Arturo was drinking a bottle of beer. He looked completely unfazed by their day.

Darcy held up her hand to admire her ring. 'When I tell people at work next week that this is what I spent twenty-four hours doing, I doubt if anyone will believe me.'

'You have the ring, and the photos to prove it. Why wouldn't they?'

She sighed and looked out across the Rome skyline. 'Because it's just not a very Darcy thing to do,' she admitted.

'But you're enjoying yourself?' His phone pinged, but he ignored it.

'Of course I'm enjoying myself,' she said. 'I just couldn't have imagined doing anything like this.' She gave a huge appreciative sigh as she looked at the elegant structure of the sunset-lit Colosseum again. 'And I definitely picked the right city and...' She hesitated, wondering if she should say it out loud. She raised her glass of water. 'And I definitely picked the right Italian to come along for the ride.'

His eyebrows raised. He was good at that—it was his signature move. 'Just the right Italian, not the right guy?'

'Oh...' She laughed. 'You're going to be like that then?'

'Like what?' he said with a gleam in his eye.

The waiter came over and set down their plates of salted cod, alongside courgette flowers with mozzarella. The portions looked small on the plate, but as soon as she started eating, Darcy realised how filling the dish was. The waiter also brought a bottle of chilled white wine and they ate in a leisurely fashion, taking their time, until the sun had completely set and a dark sky filled with a smattering of stars was above them.

'Did you order pasta?' she whispered across the table.

He nodded and she leaned back with her hand on her stomach. 'I'm not sure if I can.'

'How about I ask for a half portion?' He smiled. 'You really want to taste this pasta.'

'Can't be in Italy and not taste the pasta,' she said with a smile, taking a second to savour the moment.

She was unbelievably lucky. She knew she was. 'This day has been perfect.' She sighed. 'I think I'll still remember it when I'm old and grey.'

'You, grey? Never.'

She touched her hair. 'That's the thing about blonde. It hides the grey better.'

'You can't know that?' he joked.

She laughed as she took a small sip of wine. 'Not yet, but my mother told me.'

He raised his glass towards her. 'And our mothers know everything.'

She leaned forward. 'Tell me a bit about your family. They must be very proud of you.'

'Sometimes,' he said with a hint of humour. 'My mother both likes and dislikes that I do the same job as my father. She supported my studies, and the fact I travel so much for work, but the truth is, she would like me at home. There's much work to be done on the estate, and while I love the place...' he paused and took a deep breath '... I'm not ready to do that yet.'

'Could you work from home? Isn't that what everyone does now?'

He paused for a moment, clearly trying to find the right words. That made her instantly curious. 'My work is sometimes…intense. There are too many distractions at home. And that doesn't include my mother and my sister. Edinburgh gave me the change of scene that I needed.'

'I can relate to that,' she said with a smile, without explaining any further. 'What does your sister do?'

He smiled back. It was clear he had great affection for his younger sister. Darcy liked that. Even though her relationship with her sister was a little fractured now, family was important to her.

'Cara has done a number of things. She studied design and then started with one of the Italian fashion houses. She was doing well, but got into a certain rivalry with a colleague.'

'That sounds like a film or some kind of juicy novel.'

He gave a soft laugh and nodded. 'It could have been. Then things happened with my father, and she decided to leave. Right now, she helps my mother run the estate. She's excellent at it. Probably because she has a gift for systems, processes and, usually, people.'

'Is this a simple way of saying *Don't cross my sister*?'

There was a flicker of panic in his face, and for an instant she felt her cheeks flame. Of course she would never meet Arturo's sister. She hadn't meant to imply that.

Thankfully, the waiter appeared to set down their main courses. She thought he would leave it, and let the conversation naturally drift in another direction, but he didn't. He looked her straight in the eye.

'You would never need to worry about Cara. She would like you just as much as I do. My sister knows what's important to me.'

For a second she wondered if she'd heard right. One moment her heart had been plummeting, thinking she'd made a silly faux pas, but now...? Now, she was getting an entirely different message.

Her throat was instantly dry, even though her mouth should be watering with the aroma of pasta and meat sauce beneath it. She was kind of flabbergasted. Although they'd danced together, been up close and personal, even held hands today on a number of occasions, their friendship hadn't progressed any further. They still barely knew each other. But that didn't mean that the sparks weren't obvious. Of course he was attractive.

But Darcy wasn't sure she was ready to trust anyone again. Arturo had a distinct hint of mystery about him. She was sure there was much more to him than met the eye. Plus, there was the fact they moved in different circles. Arturo had never flung it in her face, but his casual comments about his office, where he was staying in Edinburgh, and the family estate in Verona made her know that money wasn't an issue for him.

Whilst she was financially independent and happy to be, she didn't have millions in the bank, and didn't aspire to either. She had an awful feeling that his sister might see someone like her as a potential money-grabber, and Darcy was too proud to let anyone treat her like that.

She gave a small smile. 'If we are talking about sisters, maybe I should warn you about mine.'

'Warn me? That doesn't sound good.'

Darcy held up her hand. 'Fizz is fabulous. But she can be intense.' She pulled out her phone and turned it round so he could see a range of texts. 'I sent her a picture earlier of us, saying that I loved Rome, and let's just say I've been inundated.'

'You never mentioned that we'd met?'

Darcy swallowed. Was he hurt? Finally, she came out with, 'I wasn't sure what to tell her.'

If he was offended at all, he didn't let it show. His voice was smooth. 'You could have told her you'd met a handsome Italian man at dance class, who waltzed you around the place as if you were floating on air.' He had a wide smile on his face.

'You're already taking this too far,' she said as she bent to sample some of the pasta.

'You could have said that we agreed to do a mad twenty-four hours together, and I was going to be your—what do you call it?—right-hand man?'

She thought he would stop but he continued. 'You could have told her we'd been for drinks, or that I'd seen your house.'

Darcy held up her hand. 'And if I'd told her all of these things there is a chance she would have demanded to meet you.'

'And that would be bad, how?'

Darcy laughed. 'She'd want to know name, age, place of birth, friends, family, job, intentions, past history, and even music and food tastes. Then,' she added with a wave of her fork, 'she would have asked for references.'

'Sounds a bit like Cara, to be honest,' he said easily.

'Then maybe they could be a good match.

They could spark off each other, whilst we just got on with it.'

'And leave us alone?' he asked with a small rise of his eyebrows.

She licked her lips, taking a sip of her wine and saying playfully, 'If we wanted to be.'

The night was closing in around them. Darcy had thought she would be tired by this point— exhausted even. But she wasn't. Not while she was in Arturo's company. Something inside was keeping her going. A buzz. Biology told her it was pure adrenaline. But for Darcy it was about being around someone she felt a connection with.

He leaned forward. 'How do you feel about going to a club in Rome?'

Her eyes narrowed for a second. 'What kind of club?'

'A nightclub.' He smiled. 'There will be dancing, just not the ballroom kind.'

'Dubious dancing?' she asked cautiously.

Arturo laughed out loud. 'I think my sister would always call my dancing dubious.' But he clearly knew what she meant. 'Don't worry.' He reached over the table and touched her hand. 'All will be above board. You might even like it.'

There it was, that gleam in his eye again. The one that meant she found it really difficult to say no. She heard his phone ping but, as before, Arturo just ignored it. It seemed he knew who was messaging, and was in no hurry to reply.

They finished their wine, Arturo paid the bill and then he took her by the hand, leading her down some narrow streets. The walk was longer than expected, but the night was balmy and it was pleasant to see the streets of Rome while it wasn't so hot, and so busy.

There was a line outside the nightclub, but Arturo walked to the front and exchanged a few words with one of the stewards, who stood aside and gestured them both inside.

Even before they descended the stairs, Darcy could feel the music reverberate around them. She put her hand on the wall as it vibrated next to her. She grinned. 'This place is bouncing,' she said.

He nodded, smiling back. 'Best nightclub in Rome, best music, best DJs.'

The next few hours passed in a dark blur. The music was fantastic. Darcy had visited nightclubs when she'd been younger with her sisters and friends. But when Laura had become ill, all that had stopped. They'd all been worried because Laura was immunosuppressed. They didn't want to take a chance of bringing anything more serious than a cold home.

Because Darcy had been focused on work

for the last few years, nightclubs hadn't been her thing. She didn't sit at home every night. She'd gone to the Edinburgh Festival Fringe a few times, and to the theatre to see various touring shows.

But here? Now? It was all about having fun with her handsome companion. Whilst neither of them was a self-confessed dance lover, in this environment they both came alive.

The beat of the music let them bounce when they had to bounce, groove a little when the tempo changed, and Arturo had hidden smooth moves when the music slowed to something more intimate.

As Darcy wrapped her hands around his neck, he put his hands at her waist, pulling her closer whilst whispering in her ear. 'So, what do you think of Rome?'

She tipped her head up towards his. 'Everything has been beyond my expectations so far.'

They'd been together all day. Not only had a nightclub been the last place she'd expected to be, she was still wearing her black capri pants, white tied shirt and flat shoes. It was hardly nightclub attire. But being with Arturo made her forget about the little things. Years ago, she would have spent hours picking an outfit for a nightclub. She would have spent even longer fixing her hair and make-up. She'd walked in here without even giving it a thought. Having Arturo's hand in hers, his skin touching hers was hypnotic, and made her not worry about things she would have considered before.

'We have one more thing to do before it's time to catch our flight home,' he said, his lips brushing against her ear. 'Are you ready for the next step?'

Her heart fluttered, her mind immediately going someplace else. It could just be his choice of words, but what did the next step mean to him? Because she could think of a million things it might mean to her.

They climbed the stairs, back out into the cooler night air. It was the early hours of the morning, but the streets weren't empty. It seemed that Rome was the city that never slept.

Hand in hand, they walked casually down a few streets to an open café. 'Coffee?' he suggested.

She gave a nod and he ordered them coffees and panettone, and they walked along the street nibbling their cake and sipping their coffees. It had been a good choice as the coffee warmed her again, and the panettone filled with fruit revived her a little.

As they disposed of their cups, Arturo gave her a sideways glance. 'Do you recognise where we are?'

Darcy looked around, scanning the street and shops and restaurants. With their shutters down it was hard to identify what part of the city they were in. She wanted to pull out her phone to try and get her bearings, but she trusted Arturo and just gave a shake of her head. 'Not a clue,' she admitted.

He took her hand again and stood in front of her. 'I wanted to bring you full circle,' he said.

'What does that mean?'

'Come on.' They walked along one more street and she was struck by the fact there were even more people around here. As they rounded the corner, she gave a little gasp.

They were back at the Trevi Fountain. At night, it looked very different. White and blue lights highlighted the whole space. The backdrop seemed brighter and more stark, the water in the fountains even more blue. It had a magical quality to it that hadn't quite been there in the heat of the day.

There were still some people around. The fountain in the middle of the night was obviously some kind of not so hidden secret in Rome. The constant trickle of running water was peaceful, almost hypnotic.

Arturo steered them over to a spot to sit, and as they settled he put his arm around her. A couple in front of them were throwing in their coins, lost in their own private moment.

Darcy relaxed into Arturo. She reached up to grasp his hand on her shoulder. 'This was a great final spot,' she said, then gave him a sceptical glance. 'You could have mentioned this before.'

'And spoil our happy ending?' he joked, and her stomach flipped. 'Anyhow, it was a good place to visit earlier, because then you could appreciate the contrast at this time of night.'

She heard him take a deep breath, and instantly her stomach clenched. 'So, I'm going to ask you something on the way home, and it's really important that I'm honest with you before I ask.'

'This sounds serious.'

He gave a sad kind of smile, but didn't actually give an answer. He took another deep breath. 'You know that I told you I was like Indiana Jones.'

She smiled instantly. 'Yes, it has kind of played on my mind.'

He pressed his lips together. 'I take it you've watched the movies?'

'Hasn't everyone?'

He gave the slightest of nods. 'In that case—' his eyes fixed over towards the fountain '—you'll remember that Indiana Jones got into trouble sometimes. He got chased. People didn't like him.'

She almost laughed. 'Only the bad guys.'

He turned to look at her. 'Well, in my line of work, there can be bad guys.'

Her skin instantly chilled. 'What do you mean?'

'I mean that, on occasion, I get threatened. My job can make me unpopular—usually because I'm retrieving things that have been stolen, that don't belong to the people that currently own them. And sometimes, for me, and I think for my dad too, things can be a bit dangerous.'

'Like getting chased by a giant rock?' She was grasping at straws and it was the first thing she could think of.

He gave a soft laugh. 'No, I've never been chased by a giant rock. But I just want to be honest with you. I get threatened sometimes.' He ran his fingers through his dark hair. 'My family have never been threatened, I wouldn't let any of my friends get threatened, my fiancée was never threatened.'

'Your what?' Her heart had just stopped beating.

He winced. 'Faye,' he said without hesitation. 'She was in the same line of work. She died five years ago, in Japan. A road accident. Nothing to do with either of our jobs.'

'You were engaged?' She just had to say the words out loud to make herself process them.

To his credit, he didn't look abashed at all. 'Yes, I was. It's been five years since she died.'

It was Darcy's turn to suck in a deep breath. 'Oh, I'm so sorry.' She reached over and put her hand on his chest. She'd thought what had happened to her was bad. But this? It didn't bear thinking about. No wonder she'd thought Arturo seemed a little guarded around her. He'd had all this weight on his shoulders.

'There's never really a good time to say that, is there?' he asked.

Her stomach flip-flopped as she thought of what she hadn't told him. She gave him a sad smile. 'Not really, but you've done it. And I'm glad you have. I'm glad you told me.' She leaned back against him because she meant it. She was glad to know. It gave her a bigger picture to look at and consider.

But this news was huge. Maybe because she'd told him about Laura, he'd felt as if he should share about Faye. And he'd said it had been nothing to do with their jobs—but there had also been that other news that his job could be dangerous. How did a handsome Italian, with a partly dangerous job, end up at the same dance class as her in Edinburgh? Honestly, if she was writing a script for a film, she would never have thought of this.

Even though she wanted to ask a million questions, this beautiful setting was just not the time and place. She didn't want to put him on the spot. Indeed, she had no right to. She'd invited him here as someone to show her around a city in Italy. It had been convenient for her. And if she kept telling herself that, she could ignore that underlying pull towards him, and that obvious wave of attraction.

He held her gaze for a second, and she wondered if he was gauging her reaction. Was he happy she'd been accepting, or was he curious she hadn't bombarded him with questions? But Arturo seemed as unruffled as ever. He gave her a smile. One that danced down the nerves in her spine. So sexy…

Then he pointed over to the right side of the fountain. 'See that over there?'

She squinted as she followed his finger and nodded when she worked out where he was pointing. 'What is it?'

'It's called the Fountain of Love. Two simple water spouts that cross before landing together in the stone basin below.' His voice was deep and low. 'Legend has it that if two lovers drink from the crossing spouts together, they will remain in love for ever.'

It was as if someone froze the world around them. Their gazes were locked together. Darcy licked her lips. 'But we're not lovers.'

There was a soft smile on Arturo's lips. 'Not yet,' he said in a whisper. Darn, this man was sexy. 'But everyone has to start somewhere. How about with a kiss?'

A light breeze blew across her skin. She could have sworn it was just to make all the hairs on her skin stand on end.

She swallowed, then smiled. 'I think we could start there,' she said.

He bent his head towards her, his lips brushing against hers at first, before his hand moved gently behind her head and slid through her hair. Now he was kissing her, his lips firm but still gentle. She didn't even want to consider where Arturo had practised his technique— she just wanted to applaud anyone that had come before—and had helped him reach his current state of perfection. Because in this current state of perfection he was hers.

She angled her body more towards his, still sitting on the steps. Her hand slid up the front of his shirt and he gave a little groan.

Arturo pulled her closer, intensifying their kiss. His hand moved from the back of her head to the side of her face. His fingertip touch was butterfly-light, touching her cheek, her ear, then running down her neck and making her gasp for air.

For a few moments, nothing else mattered. Nothing bad had ever happened in her life, or in his. She was floating in a pink fluffy cloud, with the most gorgeous man focusing all his attention on her. Her lips were in heaven, other parts of her body were coming to life and urging for more. She couldn't remember a kiss ever doing this to her.

There was a shout to the side of them that sadly jolted her back to reality.

She laughed and leaned back. Another couple next to them—the one who must have shouted—gave a round of applause and Darcy could feel heat rush into her cheeks. Arturo gave them an amused nod and pulled her up, walking her over to the Fountain of Love, which was a little more secluded.

They paused above the two water spouts. 'Ready?' he asked.

'You're sure we can drink this?' she countered.

'Live a little,' was his wicked reply, and she flicked a little of the water at him, before they both bent to drink from the spouts.

'Remind me what this means?' she asked, wiping her chin.

'Apparently, it guarantees love and faithfulness.'

'Just for lovers?' She was teasing, but she couldn't help it.

'Who knows?' He gave a playful shrug. 'Guess we'll need to find out.'

He glanced at his watch, and she knew what would come next. Already she could sense the sky starting to lighten in gradual elements around them.

She stepped forward again and took his hands. 'Thank you. Thank you for coming with me and showing me all the best parts of Rome.'

He released one hand so he could put his arm around her, guiding her away from the Fountain of Love and back towards the main road, where they could hail a taxi.

'It's been my pleasure. But I did warn you that I might ask for something in return.'

'Oh, yes. What?' She was in a good mood and was relaxed, still recovering from that first kiss. Her lips still tingled.

'Come with me to my sister's wedding.'

Her footsteps faltered. 'What?'

'I need a partner for my sister's wedding. Who better than the person I'm dancing with?

Who better than the person I've just spent twenty-four hours in Rome with?'

She wrinkled her nose. 'You've made your sister sound kind of terrifying.'

He laughed. 'Cara would love that you said that! But I refuse to tell her. Come with me. Meet my family. See the estate. I promise you, once you've seen an Italian wedding, nothing else will compare.'

She looked at him warily. 'Why do I think there's a little bit more to this?'

He gave the smallest shrug, but nodded. 'I've warned you about my family. They can be a little full-on. Now my sister's getting married, their attention will fully be on—' He lifted his hand to his chest, and Darcy finished the sentence for him.

'You.'

He nodded. 'I fear they may have a dozen lovely Italian daughters and nieces of friends lined up to try and pair me off with.'

'So, what am I? Your protection?'

He laughed out loud, his face breaking into a wide smile. 'Absolutely. If I'm there with you, then they won't try and pair me off with anyone else.'

A little part of her wondered if she should be offended by this ask. He was using her as a mechanism of convenience—just like she'd done when she'd asked him to come to Rome. Could she really say no, when he'd also opened up about other parts of his life too? Should she second-guess the kiss they'd just shared? Was it all just part of a bribe?

No. She pushed that out of her head. She wasn't going to let that perfect kiss be spoiled by her brain overthinking.

'When is it?' asked Darcy.

'It's in one week. Will you have problems getting time off work?'

'Oh, no.' She shook her head. 'I'm owed about a million holidays anyhow. Time off won't be the problem. Finding something to wear to your sister's wedding might be.'

'You can borrow something of hers,' he said nonchalantly.

She shook her head, laughing. 'You just don't get the girl thing, do you?'

'What?' he asked without a care in the world, waving to a taxi cab.

'I'll come,' she said, before she could change her mind, or talk herself out of it. 'But let me pick my own outfit.'

The taxi pulled up and Arturo opened the door for her. He bowed. 'Your wish is my command,' he joked as she climbed in.

Darcy sank into the seat, fatigue starting to come over her in waves. By the time Arturo had climbed in beside her and put his arm around her again, her eyes wouldn't stay open.

'Sleep,' he said softly. And she leaned against him, wondering if this whole day had actually just been part of a dream.

CHAPTER EIGHT

'BUT WHO IS HE?' pressed Fizz.

'I told you. Arturo Fabiano. I met him at a dance class. He came to Rome with me. You've seen him. I sent you a picture.'

'But that's all you've sent. And you never mentioned him before you sent that picture. Now you're going to his sister's wedding with him at his estate in Verona? Who is this guy?'

Fizz said the words with such indignation that Darcy wanted to laugh out loud.

Darcy shrugged her shoulders. 'Don't read too much into things. It's kind of an arrangement of convenience. He helped me tick off something on my bucket list, and I'll help fend off all the Italian women his mother and sister will try and throw at him. He's just an Italian staying in Edinburgh. He's a sort of modern-day Indiana Jones.'

'That's the most dubious job description I've heard in a long time,' shot back Fizz. Then she frowned. 'Are you sure he's not making that up?'

Darcy leaned back and smiled. 'Well, if he is it's a great story.'

Fizz pointed her finger. 'There. You're doing that thing.'

'What thing?'

Fizz waved her hand. 'That thing you do when you get all starry-eyed about someone.' She looked as if she was going to go further, but paused and clearly pulled herself back. 'I don't think this is a convenience thing for you. You've not done that for a long time.'

There was silence between them. They both knew the last time Darcy had been starry-eyed. It had ended in disaster.

'Anyway,' said Darcy quickly, 'I need something to wear to his sister's wedding. Any suggestions? Or where should I get something? It's been so long since I've bought an outfit like that I don't know where to shop any more.'

Fizz sat drumming her fingers on her desk for a few moments. She was clearly contemplating something. After a second, her eyes brightened. 'Actually, I've just thought of the perfect thing.'

'What?'

Fizz shook her head. 'I bought it last year.

Never had a chance to wear it. It will look gorgeous on you, and it's perfect for a wedding.'

'Promise me it's not a bikini,' said Darcy cautiously. She knew how mischievous her sister could be.

But Fizz looked sincere. 'Honestly, it will be perfect. I'll pack it up and send it twenty-four-hour delivery.'

'Thanks. Are you going to give me a hint?'

Fizz's smile widened. 'Not at all.'

Darcy paused for a moment. 'Hey, how's Oli?' Fizz bristled. It was odd, she and Oli had been friends for ever. 'Didn't you two have plans for something?'

'Yeah, well, maybe. I'm not sure.'

Darcy was surprised. She'd always thought Oliver was secretly in love with Fizz and would do anything she asked. But maybe things had changed. They hadn't had a proper conversation about Oli in a while.

'I have a few things to sort out,' said Fizz, and Darcy wasn't sure if she was talking about life, the dress heading her way, or Oli.

'Hey.' Darcy smiled at her sister. 'Remember, we're the Bennetts—we can do anything.'

Fizz's face broke into a smile, slightly sad at first, then broadening. She gave a smile. 'You're right. Watch out for the post. Let me know what you think when it arrives, okay?'

Darcy nodded and signed off. Was everything all right with her sister? She didn't like to pry, and if something was wrong, Fizz would tell her, wouldn't she?

CHAPTER NINE

ARTURO'S PHONE HAD literally not stopped ringing since he'd finally arrived back from Rome and responded to the original message. Sleep hadn't been an option, and he'd spoken to discreet colleagues around the world in an attempt to authenticate the item he would soon try to retrieve.

In between this, he'd broken it to his mother and sister that he would be bringing a guest to the wedding. He didn't need to worry if Cara would attempt an internet search of Darcy, since she'd done it while they were on their video call and spun her tablet around to show him.

'Ooh, she's clever. And she's listed as working at a few major companies. That's good, isn't it?' Then Cara frowned, a suspicious gleam in her eye. 'Or does that mean she changes jobs before she's found out?'

'Found out for what?'

'Found out for not being able to do the job she actually got.'

'Cara—' his sister flinched at his warning tone, then was clearly amused '—I'm telling you right now, concentrate on your wedding. Leave my date alone.'

'Your date? Is that how you're describing her? Not your girlfriend. Or your new love interest.'

'Cara,' he warned again, 'don't you have a million other details to worry about? Like the position of the sun in the sky? Or which way the wind might blow?'

His sister's face tightened. Yes, he knew her that well. She was an absolute perfectionist. Living in Edinburgh whilst she'd been planning her wedding had likely been a blessing in disguise.

His mother's face filled the frame and she pushed Cara from the chair. There was no malice in it. His mother had probably had her fill of Cara for the last few weeks, and when Arturo checked in she liked to give him her full attention.

'Well, I can't wait to meet your date. I'm sure she'll be absolutely charming.'

Arturo started to breathe a little easier. 'She may seem a little shy at first.'

'I thought all English girls were brash and outspoken.'

Arturo bristled instantly until he caught the

amused glance on his mother's face. He took a breath. 'We've spent some time together. I like her. She lost a sister five years ago and…' He slowed. 'I suspect she's not quite over things.'

His mother gave an understanding nod. 'She might not be quite ready for a family like ours,' she said good-naturedly. Then, with more caution, 'Or a man like yourself.'

'What does that mean?'

'It means that it sounds like she may need some nurturing, some support.'

'And you think I can't do that?' He was wounded that his mother thought so little of him.

'I suspect—' her voice was even '—that your job might not allow for that. You leave at a moment's notice. You can be out of touch for days. Does she understand that yet?'

He swallowed. 'We haven't got that far. I did give her a little warning about my job.'

His mother gave a tiny bow of her head and put her hand on her heart. 'I loved your father dearly and he loved me, but he also loved his work.' She gave a gentle smile. 'You are your father's son. I don't think you ever really understood how much I hated the fact his job took him away, or that on occasion it put him, or even us, in danger.' She looked her son directly in the eye. 'And I would never have forgiven him if anything had happened to any of you.'

Arturo's skin prickled. His mother had never spoken like this. She'd never revealed this part of her marriage. And whilst it made him uncomfortable, he understood why she was doing it.

'Arturo,' she continued with a wave of her hand, 'you know that in my secret plans I have you settling down with the nice Italian girl and coming back to stay here for the rest of your life.' She gave him a warm smile. 'But I also know that the life I have in my head for you and the life you have in your head for yourself are two entirely different things.' She took a deep breath. 'I only want you to be happy. I am delighted you've found someone you want to bring to Cara's wedding. I only ask that you think carefully about the girl you've found, whether you are right for each other, and whether you can give her what she needs.'

He was glad he was sitting down because this was the most insightful conversation he'd ever had with his mother. They didn't talk about people and feelings—not even when Faye had died, or his father had died. They talked about business, other family and running the estate. But those conversations had been perfunctory. This was entirely different.

'You haven't mentioned what *I* might need,' he said, knowing exactly how his mother would react to that.

His mother gave a gentle laugh. 'And that's where our conversation ends. I don't need to know what you need. I'm sure you can work that out for yourself.' She gave a wave and the conversation finished, just as Arturo had predicted.

He stood and stretched his back, looking out over the city skyline. He still wondered how on earth he'd ended up in Edinburgh. Even though the city had captured his heart, he now wondered if something else had pulled him there. Was this just fate? Did he even believe in that?

His phone pinged again and he sighed. He still had work to complete, and a dance class to get to. He smiled. Margaret had better wave a magic wand at some point in the next few days or this could all get messy.

CHAPTER TEN

'I THOUGHT THERE would be other people here,' Darcy said as she stripped off her jacket and changed into her dance shoes.

Arturo smiled. 'There's another class in an hour. But I paid Margaret for some private tuition for us. I've still not got all the steps and I'm running out of time fast.'

Darcy put a hand on her hip. 'You could just sway around the dance floor. Other couples do that and...' she gave him a little smile '...you managed that the other night.'

He pulled a face, walked over and put his hand over hers, anchoring it on her hip. She automatically smiled and took a step closer as he spoke. 'That's okay for an actual couple. But for the guy playing Father of the Bride, it looks a bit stupid. I have to at least manage a few steps.'

'And how many have you actually mastered?' Margaret's voice made them both jump as she walked up behind them.

'The natural turn, the backward change with the left foot and the reverse turn.' Darcy jumped in quickly to save him.

He gave her a nod as Margaret rolled her eyes. 'Only halfway then? You still need to do the chasse change steps and the backward change with the left foot. Come on then, I'll help you master the rest.'

The next hour flew past. They only ended up on a heap on the floor once, when Arturo mistimed his steps a little too enthusiastically. But they were definitely getting better.

'You have improved,' said Margaret encouragingly. Then she winked at Darcy. 'He's gone from absolutely terrible to merely diabolical.'

Arturo opened his mouth to defend himself, but Margaret was laughing. 'We'll cover the Viennese waltz for the first half hour of the next class. Stay and practice. You're actually getting there.' She tapped Arturo's arm. 'We'll make a dancer of you yet.'

Once the rest of the participants filed in they continued dancing, concentrating on their steps until they'd mastered all the basics and things were starting to feel a bit smoother.

'I think we might have it,' whispered Darcy excitedly.

'But will I remember any of it tomorrow?' groaned Arturo.

'I think I know a way to imprint it on your brain so you don't forget,' joked Darcy.

'What?' He actually looked hopeful.

She nodded. 'Picture your sister's face if you get it wrong.'

He shuddered, and smiled. 'Yes, that will do it.'

'Hey,' he remarked, twirling her around. 'That's two items ticked off your bucket list. What's going to be your third?'

'I haven't had much of a chance to think about it yet.'

'Remind me what it is.' He had one hand resting on her hip and the other holding her hand. They were still up close and personal in the dance position and for the first time since they'd kissed she felt a little awkward.

The words seemed to stick in her throat as she said them out loud. 'The third thing was to make a commitment to someone or something—it has to be important, something that lasts a few years.'

He frowned. 'Your sister thought you had issues with making commitments?'

Darcy honestly wasn't sure how to answer that. There were still elements of her past that she hadn't shared with him, and she wasn't sure she wanted to.

He had the strangest look on his face, and

did she imagine it or had his body just tensed a little?

A thought flooded into her brain. Oh, no. Did he think she was talking about them?

Her legs wobbled. What if he thought she was just making things up, and had thrown this bucket list item in for other reasons?

She pulled her hands away from his and wiped them on her skirt. 'I think we're done now. Margaret's getting ready to change the class onto the next dance.'

Arturo looked as if he had barely drawn a breath and she wasn't sure what to make of it. He blinked and then coughed, breaking his gaze from hers and turning to look around the room.

'Sure,' he murmured.

As they got their coats and made their way outside, Darcy reached inside her bag and pulled out the envelope that contained her bucket list. 'Here,' she said, not considering the handwritten notes that were there.

His brow wrinkled and he took the envelope from her hand and drew out the letter, unfolding it. His eyes widened as he realised what it was.

'The whole bucket list?' he asked.

'The whole bucket list,' she repeated.

His head tipped to the side by the tiniest angle.

'Why would you share this with me?' There was something about his words, and his tone.

'Because I told you the third item inside, and I wasn't sure if you believed me.'

It struck her that until that second she hadn't realised how important it was to her that Arturo *did* believe her. And that scared her.

'Of course I believed you.' His words were barely a whisper. She knew he was reading the rest of what was written on her letter. But he lifted his head with a clear expression on his face.

'Your sister gave you a bucket list. She gave you some hints and other comments. But you have to interpret this *your* way. Not hers. And if you can't do it in the time frame she gave you, so what? I get you want to honour your sister, and I think that's wonderful. But you have to remember to be you. You spent your life being one of three sisters—you might feel a bit awkward about being one of two now. But you will always be you. And the Darcy Bennett that I've met is pretty great.'

He reached up with his hand and pushed a strand of her hair behind her ear. 'I even invited her to a wedding,' he said, smiling.

'A very important wedding,' she replied as she stepped forward. Her heart had stopped racing now, and her stomach was unclenching. She still didn't know Arturo very well. But now she knew for sure that she wanted that to change.

Maybe going to the wedding and meeting the family would give her the background and history part that she needed to fill in some of his blanks. While she was nervous, she was also excited. So maybe it was time to be completely honest with him.

'I've booked our flights,' he said. 'Found a dress yet?'

She raised her eyebrows. 'Fizz found me a dress.'

'That sounds promising.' It sounded more like a question than a statement.

She pulled a face. 'It is. It's just a bit more daring than I would probably have picked myself.'

'But do you like it?'

Darcy took a few moments and then nodded slowly. 'Do you know, I do. It's a beautiful dress.'

'Then be daring.' He smiled at her.

He opened the passenger door of his car. 'Jump in, let's go for a drive.'

'Where to?'

He looked down the street. 'It's still light. We'll head to the beach. Might even see the sunset.'

She climbed in. 'This could be a bad decision. Think of the last sunset you showed me. Will this one compare?'

'Beauty is in the eye of the beholder,' he said, shifting his car into gear and taking off.

Fifteen minutes later they pulled up to Portobello Beach. The sky had dimmed, but the promenade still had people walking up and down.

As they got out of the car it was clear that the wind had picked up, and Darcy's hair flew in every direction. 'Need a thicker jacket?' he called as he walked around and opened the boot of the car.

'Sure.' She nodded, her denim jacket not quite up to the blustery breeze coming off the Firth of Forth.

There were a few other people around, mainly walking dogs, as they jumped down onto the sand.

'It's been a while since I visited a beach,' she said, enjoying the wind streaming through her hair, blinking her eyes at the tiny bits of gritty sand.

'Me too,' he admitted, slinging an arm around her shoulders as they walked down to the water's edge. The first part of the sand had been soft, spongy and difficult to walk on. But as they neared the waves the sand was much firmer.

'I wonder if the tide is coming in or out?' she asked.

'Let's take some time to find out,' said Ar-

turo. It was one of his best traits. He was patient. He didn't try to rush things. They stood
together, and after a few minutes worked out
that the tide appeared to be going back out.

A little dog rushed past them, splashing them
as it bounced and sprang through the waves
with barks of pure enjoyment. Both of them
laughed, not the least bothered by the splashing. A woman rushed up next to them, another
dog on a lead in her hand. 'Scamp, come here.
Sorry.' She gave them a rueful glance. 'He just
gets so excited when he comes down here. He
loves the beach.'

Darcy wrinkled her nose. 'What kind of dog
is he?'

Arturo looked down at the other dog on the
lead. It looked a bit older. It was white and
shaggy, with short legs. 'Is that one a West
Highland terrier?'

The woman looked at him in surprise as she
picked the older dog up and tried to wrestle
Scamp back onto a lead. Darcy dropped to her
knees to help, trying to hold Scamp in place.
He still wanted to dance in the waves.

'We have no idea what Scamp is, do we, gorgeous?' the woman said, staring fondly at her
dog. 'I got them both from the dog rescue place
just outside Edinburgh.'

'They're rescue?' Darcy was surprised. She

didn't know that much about dogs and wasn't
sure what kind of dogs ended up in a rescue
centre.

The woman succeeded in getting Scamp
back on the lead and stood up, smiling. 'I've
had five dogs—not all at once, of course—but
all were rescue. I'd just lost my black Lab, and
six months later the house felt empty so I went
back along to the rescue centre. I went for one,
and came home with two.'

'How did that happen?' asked Arturo.

The woman sighed and looked fondly at her
dogs. 'They'd both been owned by an elderly
man who'd passed away unexpectedly. When
I took Scamp out of the kennels to see how
he was with me, Hugo here started whining.
They didn't like being apart. I couldn't take
one without the other.'

'You weren't worried about taking on someone else's dogs?'

'Someone else's problem, you mean?' she
asked.

Darcy nodded, embarrassed that she'd read
her mind.

'The people at the rescue centre are always
very honest about the dogs they have. These
were probably two of the best trained in there.
But most people don't want two dogs, so they'd
been overlooked.' Her smile broadened. 'Or

maybe they'd just been waiting for me.' She gave them a smile and a wave before heading off down the beach with her dogs.

As Darcy turned back, Arturo was watching her closely.

'What?' she asked.

'Nothing,' he said with a half-smile on his face.

The sun had dipped while they were talking, and he pointed at the darkening sky. 'Maybe we don't have shades of orange and the outline of the Colosseum, but I suspect Scotland's offer might be just as nice.'

'Nice?' Darcy put her hand on her hip. 'Just as well I'm an English girl and not a Scots, or I might be mortally offended by those words.'

He knew she was joking and gave her a smile. 'I can make amends.'

'How?'

He pointed to the few shops just parallel to the promenade. 'I can offer chips or ice cream.'

'They don't call it ice cream around here.'

'They don't? What do they call it?'

As they walked back up the beach, she gave him a sideways glance. 'A pokey hat.'

He almost choked. 'What?'

'It was one of the first things I learned when I got here. And I've got Arthur to thank for that.' She pulled a face. 'Although apparently the saying originated from the *other* big city in Scotland.'

'Glasgow?'

She nodded.

'I still don't get it—why on earth do they call it a pokey hat?'

'It's ice cream served in a cone, and if you turned the cone upside down it would be like a witch's hat.'

He wrinkled his nose for a few moments and shook his head. 'Does that mean you want ice cream?'

'Actually...' she grinned '... I'd rather have the chips. It's a bit cold around here.'

'Okay.'

They headed to the nearest fish and chip shop, then sat back at the beach, chips on their lap as they watched the sun finally dip in the sky.

'Hey,' she said, bumping him with her elbow. 'I've just realised that the two men I've been hanging around with most in Edinburgh are both called Arthur.'

He raised his eyebrows, but she laughed and continued. 'Arturo is the Italian form of Arthur, isn't it?'

He rolled his eyes. 'Yeah, I'll let you have that.'

She looked out across the view. 'I wonder what that means?'

'That both men you hang around with are called Arthur? Maybe their mothers just had good taste in names?'

Her eyes gleamed with mischief. 'Or maybe it's some kind of fate and I was destined to meet you both.'

Their gazes locked for a minute and neither of them spoke.

Darcy swallowed. It was now or never. Time for some honesty.

'You know how you told me about Faye, and your job?'

A wrinkle appeared in his forehead. He was surprised by the change in direction. 'Yes.'

Darcy licked her dry lips, blaming it on the wind. 'I haven't been to a wedding in five years,' she said quickly.

The wrinkle in his forehead deepened. 'None of your friends have got married?'

She shook her head. 'No—I mean yes. I've just made an excuse not to go.'

He still looked entirely baffled. 'Why?'

'Because the last wedding I went to was my own.' She said the words so quickly they all ran into each other.

His face dropped like a stone. 'You're married?'

'No.' The answer was emphatic. Then she

dropped her voice. 'I went to my wedding, but my groom didn't.'

She hated these words. She hated saying them out loud. The humiliation still felt real.

'He what?' There was a change in tone from Arturo. He looked disbelieving.

Darcy turned her head, putting her face head-on to the oncoming brisk breeze from the sea. Hopefully, that would hide the tears that were threatening to spill.

'He stood me up.' Her voice was quiet now. But Arturo had moved closer, his hand around her waist. 'He phoned me to say he wasn't coming.'

After a moment he pulled her closer, sheltering her from the wind. 'He was a damn fool, Darcy. Please tell me you don't waste a second thinking about someone like that.'

Now she did blink back tears, but brushed them away. 'I just felt like I should tell you— be honest with you, before we reach Verona.'

'In case what?' It was as if he already understood.

'In case I wobble,' she admitted.

He put both arms around her, pulling her into his chest. It felt safe this way. It felt safe to say more.

'It all worked out for the best. Ultimately, we weren't right for each other. And after a few days away, I came back and spent the next three months with my family in Bath, helping to nurse Laura. It was where I needed to be.'

'Oh, Darcy,' was all he said, one hand reaching up and cradling the back of her head.

She'd told him. It was out there, and it felt more like a relief than a humiliation.

His voice was low and considerate. 'Are you sure you want to come? You don't need to. I don't want you to do something that might make you feel uncomfortable.'

She lifted her head. 'I've avoided weddings up until now. It's time that stopped. So where better to start than at a beautiful wedding at a fabulous estate in Verona?' She put a smile on her face. 'Where I will be on my best behaviour to keep the mother of the bride, and the bride, from attempting to marry you off to some random Italian woman.'

'You're sure you'll be okay?'

She gave a gentle smile, thankful he'd been so understanding, and so kind. 'I'll be fine. A change of scenery again will be nice.' She stood up, ready to move from the breezy spot, scrunching the chip wrapper into a ball and lobbing it into a nearby bin.

His eyes widened.

'Who knows—' she grinned '—I might even surprise you.'

He stopped walking and put his hands on her shoulders. 'You do,' he said sincerely. 'Every single day.'

She stopped breathing for a second at the seriousness in his face. Was this about what she'd just told him? They'd had a few moments of sincerity. But mostly their time together had been fun and light-hearted. She knew that things might change once she met his family, and she was conjuring plans in her head about how she might introduce Arturo to Fizz, and then her mum and dad.

The fact that she was even considering those things made her know she was more hopeful about the possibility of continuing this relationship. And that scared her.

Almost as if it was a sign from the universe, Arturo locked eyes with her. He bent down to whisper in her ear, 'You surprise me every single day,' he repeated. 'And sometimes—' he straightened up and looked at her again '—you downright scare me.' The expression on his face was soft, with the hint of a smile on his lips. She knew he was still talking light-heartedly, but something inside her was squirming.

She wanted to push on. She wanted this relationship to go somewhere. But could she really expose herself to the hurt she'd had before?

A guy with a job like Indiana Jones, who was from Italy, probably a secret billionaire, and had an air of mystery about him, was hardly the best candidate for her heart. She should look for someone who would want to set down roots here, who might seem like a safer prospect, work in tech or something similar to her, and be independent but not have enough money to buy a small nation.

That would be her ideal candidate, on paper, at least.

But none of those guys had sparked her interest in the last five years. None had made her heart beat faster. None had made her excited to want to see them again. None had made her skin tingle or her lips buzz like Arturo had.

Was she just destined for heartbreak again? Maybe she should call a halt to all this. Deep down was the familiar feeling of guilt. Why should she be able to move on and take a chance at happiness when Laura had never got that chance? Was that fair?

Maybe going to the family wedding was a very bad idea. Maybe she should just rock back up to her cottage and stop imagining what the royal suite might look like in that posh Edinburgh hotel, or what size of bed it had.

But as Arturo opened the car door for her and

looked at her with those hypnotic dark brown eyes she knew she wanted to take this leap.

Even if it was a very bad idea.

Because if you didn't leap, how would you ever know where you could land?

CHAPTER ELEVEN

SHE COULD TELL Arturo was nervous. It was weird. It was not a term she'd ever associated with him. But as soon as they left Verona Airport and jumped in the sports car that was waiting for them, she could almost sense his jitters.

It could just be excitement at getting back to his home, and seeing his family again. It could be actual honest-to-goodness nerves about the upcoming wedding and his role in it. There had to be pressure on him, and she hadn't even asked if he needed to do a speech.

The Italian countryside was beautiful and the miles passed in a blur. When Arturo finally drove through a set of stone pillars with open gates, she got a real sense of what he meant by estate.

The house was not immediately visible and they continued along the curved red road for a few minutes. On one side there was open countryside, on the other, trees. Eventually the gleaming cream-coloured mansion emerged fully.

It had three floors, a fountain in front of the house and sweeping steps up to double doors. Surrounding the house were immaculate manicured gardens.

Darcy's first thought was it looked like it had been plucked from a luxury magazine. But the quiet look of the house was quickly dispelled by the number of people around. As they approached, she noticed multiple buildings on either side of the mansion, and other roads leading around the back.

A huge catering truck was parked off to one side, with another truck unloading what looked like hundreds of beautiful blooms.

Arturo didn't hesitate. He parked his sports car smack bang in front of the main door.

'Isn't there a garage?' Darcy asked dubiously.

'Serge will move it later,' he said, stepping out onto the driveway, putting his hands on his hips and taking a deep breath.

She watched with interest. After a few moments he ducked his head back down. 'Getting out, or have you changed your mind?'

'Is the air different here?'

He gave a smile. 'Everything is different here. Come on, let's embrace the chaos.'

Her nerves jangled, but she was excited too. She stepped out of the car just as the main doors opened and a man came down the steps. For some reason, she'd expected him to be in uniform. The place seemed grand enough for that. But he was wearing regular jeans and a T-shirt.

'Good to see you, Arturo,' he said easily. 'Bags in the trunk?'

Arturo's shoulders visibly relaxed. 'Nice to see you too—and yes, thanks, Serge.'

The guy gave a little nod to Darcy. 'I'll be Serge,' he joked, since Arturo had forgotten to make introductions.

'Darcy,' she said, holding out her hand, then realising that was ridiculously formal.

But Serge took it with good grace and gave her hand a firm shake. 'Nice to meet you, Darcy. I'll take your bags up to your room. If Arturo doesn't remember to tell you where it is, come and find me later, and I'll show you.'

She gave a confused smile as Arturo cut in. 'And why wouldn't I remember?'

Serge popped the boot and started pulling out the bags. He looked at Darcy and smiled. 'You want to see the size of the list Cara has for him,' he joked.

Arturo groaned.

Serge lifted all three suitcases easily. 'They

have actually made drinks for you coming. They're in the bar waiting for you both.'

Immediately, Darcy felt a little panicked and looked down at her travelling clothes. Beige cargo pants and a big white shirt. She would rather have had a chance to freshen up before she met the family.

She pushed her sunglasses up into her hair. Arturo had obviously read the panic in her face. He nodded to Serge. 'Give us two minutes.'

He walked her up the steps to the house and led her into the foyer. The floor was covered in tiny white and black tiles and a double staircase snaked up the curved interior walls. Doors left off in every direction.

Arturo took her down one corridor to a large bathroom, giving her a chance to wash her hands, tidy her hair and retouch her make-up. It only took a few minutes and he was waiting outside for her when she was done. She was already feeling swamped by the size and prestige of the place. How on earth could she fit in here? Arturo had tried to warn her that he had an 'estate', but she really hadn't grasped just *how* rich he was. She'd never mixed in this kind of circle before. The background thought that Arturo had brought her here as a convenience—to stop his family trying to pair him off with someone else—now seemed massively out of step.

'Ready?' He seemed steadier now. Maybe it was just the anticipation of being here that had made him seem nervous earlier.

She nodded, and pretended her heart wasn't pounding in her chest. He took her through another few rooms until they finally reached the room that Serge had referred to as the bar.

The Fabianos' bar was as big as any commercial bar, except it had a host of comfortable sofas and chaise longues, a few tables and chairs, a huge chandelier hanging from the ceiling and a whole wall of glass doors out to gardens with a wide array of colourful flowers.

Darcy had barely managed to take anything in before the noise erupted in the room. A woman in a coral-coloured dress with matching shoes and long dark hair stood up and flung her arms around Arturo. At first glance it was obvious they were siblings.

A graceful older woman with grey hair in a modern-cut bob and dark top and trousers came over to stand by them. She gave Darcy a kiss on the cheek. 'Delighted to meet you,' she said in perfect English. 'You must be Darcy. I'm Arturo's mother, but please call me Maria.'

'Thank you,' said Darcy, watching as Arturo's

sister finally unravelled herself from her brother. She spun around towards Darcy.

Cara was stunning, with the same dark eyes as her brother and a warm complexion. She gave Darcy a slightly more chaste hug, then kissed both her cheeks. 'Cara,' she said. 'Welcome to our home.'

Darcy glanced around nervously. There was a handsome man standing behind Cara, and Cara pulled him forward. 'This is my fiancé, Dante.'

Dante stepped forward, shook her hand and kissed her cheek. 'How about a drink?' he said, as if he could sense her nerves.

The long bar had a variety of drinks already prepared. 'What do you like? A cocktail? Espresso martini? Strawberry daiquiri? Limoncello? Or some wine?'

Arturo walked over and helped himself to a chilled bottle of beer and Darcy picked up a strawberry daiquiri. The glass had condensation on it, and the first sip of the drink was pleasantly chilled.

Arturo led them over to a firm sofa to sit next to his family. As they started to chat, they drifted between a mixture of Italian and English. Clearly, they were speaking English for her benefit, but it was fascinating the way they all switched easily between languages. There

were a few spirited exchanges between the siblings, but they were all in Italian and Darcy
made a note to ask Arturo what they were spar-
ring about later.

She relaxed into the sofa, her eyes occasionally caught by movement outside in the grounds.
Off to the left, a large marquee had been set
up in the garden. It was bigger than any she'd
seen before and was already set with tables and
chairs. A large archway of pink and white roses
framed an arbour that made Darcy wonder if it
was being set up for the photographs.

As the conversation slowed next to her, she
turned towards Cara. 'Everything looks so
beautiful. You are so lucky to be getting married in a place that you love.'

Cara tilted her elbow towards Darcy. 'Let me
give you the full tour.'

Arturo shot her a worried glance, but his
sister gave him a look that only a sister could,
and Darcy couldn't see any way out of this.

She smiled, slid her arm through Cara's and
let her lead her around the house. Cara was
charm itself, self-confident, intelligent, but with
a definite hint of something else. Her coral silk
dress was exquisite and clung to her perfect
figure. She had long lashes, beautiful skin and
even her nails were flawless. Darcy had never
been the type of person to compare herself

to someone else, but every now and then she sensed that Cara was looking at her clothes, her haircut, her nails… Or maybe she was just being entirely paranoid.

As they walked around the house, Darcy got a true feel for the extent of the property and land that the Fabiano family owned. She lost count of the number of bedrooms and bathrooms in the house. The larger suites had bedrooms, dressing rooms, sitting rooms and en suite bathrooms of their own. The kitchen that the staff worked in was a gleaming stainless-steel ensemble. The storage facilities for food seemed larger than any restaurant's.

There was a library, an honest-to-goodness ballroom, multiple sitting rooms and an orangery with a curved glass dome at the back of the house.

Cara pointed out parts of the grounds—the garages, stables, swimming pool and pool house, tennis courts and staff residences. All the while she gently plied Darcy with questions.

How had she met Arturo? How well did she know him? Had he told her about his job? What did Darcy do? What exactly was a cybersecurity job? Where did she live? Did she have children? Had she been married before?

The last question had thrown her, and she'd

stumbled over it and been met with a tiny look
of suspicion. Darcy should have expected it.
She was twenty-nine. Lots of women of her
age had been married before. It wasn't exactly
an outrageous question. But she just hadn't
expected it. Was it possible Arturo had said
something about her to his family?

Cara spoke easily, her English had an Italian
lilt to it that was hypnotic. But Darcy's stomach remained half clenched the whole time.
Maybe she was a bit tired from the journey. If
there had been a chance to wash and change
she might have felt a bit brighter. Instead, she
felt slightly under the microscope.

By the time they returned to the bar she was
absolutely relieved to see Arturo again—and
by the look on his face he was equally relieved
to see her. He offered to take her up to her room
and she accepted with a smile.

'Thought your sister had taken me captive
somewhere?' she teased as they walked up the
stairs.

'It crossed my mind,' he admitted.

'Are you okay?' she asked.

'Of course,' he said immediately, and it made
her a tiny bit nervous.

Two minutes later he showed her to her room,
with a large bed and bathroom and beautiful
views of the impeccable gardens. From here,

she could even see where the wedding festivities were being set up, and it was a real hive of activity.

'We're not sharing?' she asked, then wanted to slap herself for coming out with that.

It was forward, and ridiculous. Their relationship hadn't changed to that level yet. She was clearly tired or she would never have said that.

Arturo looked amused. 'You're welcome in my room any time you like. Even though my mother and sister will spot you on CCTV, or by the hidden alarms in the house, and likely make you meet our family lawyer on the spot.'

He must have recognised the horror on her face because he reached over and touched her arm. 'I'm joking. I didn't want to presume something, or make my mother ask questions you might not have wanted. I thought you might want some space to yourself once you meet the billion Italian relatives that will be attending tomorrow. Do you want me to move you?'

She shook her head. 'No, of course not, and thank you.'

He'd been courteous and gentlemanly. How would she have really felt if she'd just been shown into his rooms with no conversation about it? So why, oh, why did she feel the tiniest bit offended? She shook it off.

'Want some time to wash and change before dinner tonight?'

She raised her eyebrow. 'The dinner you forgot to tell me about?' She then gave a grateful smile. 'I'd love it.'

'Will I send you some food up meantime?'

Her smile widened. 'Go on then.' She patted her stomach. 'I think I'd better try and soak up the cocktails from downstairs.'

He paused for a moment then gave her a look. 'Everything will be fine,' he reassured. 'My family love you already.'

As he walked out and closed the door behind him Darcy swallowed nervously and sat down at the window seat. Strangely, she wasn't entirely reassured. And if she knew Arturo at all, from the expression on his face, neither was he.

Arturo was restless. He could already sense the vibe from his family. It wasn't that they didn't like Darcy. This was his fault. He'd sprung her on them at short notice. And while it had seemed like a good idea at the time, now, he wasn't so sure.

She'd looked nervy and jangly when she'd come back from the walk with his sister. He wondered what Cara had said. She had a gift for sometimes saying things without actually saying them. She also had a face that could express a thousand words. And he only hoped she hadn't made Darcy feel unwelcome, although he was certain she would never do that deliberately.

Or maybe it was the estate. He hadn't really gone into a lot of details with Darcy before they'd got here. Maybe the size of the place overwhelmed her. She had known about his office space, and about where he was staying in Edinburgh. Both places were clearly expensive, but he had never hinted at how much his family were worth. The cost of the office space, or hotel bill in Edinburgh, would easily be covered by the interest the family accounts made in only one day.

Tonight's meal would be a traditional sit-down family dinner, with several aunts, uncles and cousins from both sides, the groom's parents and brother, Arturo, his mother, Darcy, Cara and Dante. There would be around twenty people, which might seem a lot, but considering that another two hundred would arrive for the wedding on Sunday, it was actually minimal.

He'd forgotten to mention the dinner to Darcy at first—they'd been too busy talking about the wedding. So he'd made a few calls to ensure there would be something appropriate for her in the wardrobe to wear tonight. He'd gone for a few options and hoped she'd like something.

He walked through to the kitchen and found Rosa, one of their staff, and asked her to take some food up to Darcy. Then he made his way back through to the bar to find his sister. She was sipping a negroni at the bar, her long legs swinging as she sat on a tall stool. She shot him a smile.

'Tell me you didn't bite her.'

Cara was momentarily amused. It was their own joke. She *had* actually bitten one of their mutual friends when she'd been three years old. 'That better not be in your speech,' she warned.

He smiled easily and tapped the side of his nose. 'I'll never tell.' He moved over to his sister, 'Where's Dante?'

'He's gone to meet his parents and brother. They'll be back in time for dinner.'

He gave a slow nod, wanting—but not wanting—to ask his sister a million questions about what she thought of Darcy.

'Would you like to dance?' he said with a hint of amusement in his voice as he held his hand out to her.

The expression on her face became serious and she downed her negroni rather quickly. 'I swear if you haven't practised I will kill you,' she said. And he knew she completely meant it.

They walked through to the ballroom. It was already dressed for the evening reception tomorrow night and looked impeccable. Arturo pulled out his phone and set it on the side, music filling the room. He led her into the middle of the dance floor and bowed. Cara looked at him in surprise and gave a prompt curtsey, then they both moved into position.

He started easily, listening to the music, following the beat and picturing the steps in his mind as he did them with his feet. His sister followed smoothly. She'd probably learned the Viennese waltz in a day. Cara had always been the type of person who made dance look effortless.

He was saying the steps in his head. *Forward turn, reverse turn, forward change with left foot, backward change with left foot, and chassé, change steps.*

As the music stopped Cara stepped back, an unbelieving expression on her face, and she raised her hands and started clapping. 'I can't actually believe it. You managed it.'

'You have Margaret Scott to thank for that.' He leaned forward and whispered in her ear, 'Former world champion for the Viennese waltz, and Darcy, of course, who's been my partner.' He gave a soft smile. 'She has suffered stood-on and bruised toes on your behalf.'

Cara studied him closely. 'You like her.' It was enough. She wasn't going to ask a million questions of her brother. She was just going to ask the most important one.

'I like her,' he agreed.

'Do you love her?'

He closed his eyes. He should have known she would go there. How did he answer this question when he wasn't sure of the answer himself?

'I think I could,' he said slowly, a sweeping realisation coming over him.

Cara stepped forward and put her hand on her brother's chest. 'Have you told her?'

'About thinking I could love her, or about something else?' he asked, momentarily confused.

'About Faye, you dummy,' she said, slapping him on the chest.

He nodded. 'Yes, I've told her.'

Cara's eyebrows raised. She knew him better than he wanted to admit. 'If you've told her, does that mean you're ready to move on? Are you *ready* to love her?' Her voice was passionate, and he knew that his sister loved him fiercely and had his best interests at heart.

'I don't know,' he said, distinctly uncomfortable with this line of questioning now. 'There's something else. I know she lost her sister a few years ago. I know that was tough for her family. She revealed something else to me, just before she came here. The truth is, I'm not sure that she's ready. It feels like she might still have some walls up.'

'You'd know all about that.'

His eyes widened and he turned to his sister. She had one hand on her hip. 'What? I've been Team Arturo all my life. You've brought this girl to my wedding, Arturo. You're going to introduce her to around two hundred people tomorrow, half of whom are distant relatives of ours. You're effectively putting her under a microscope. Is she ready? You must know that as soon as I'm married, all our mother's attention will be on you.'

She shook her head and gave her brother a sympathetic look. 'I only hope you've done the right thing bringing her here. And I hope she's ready for tomorrow.'

He swallowed, knowing his sister was entirely right, and hating every second of that.

Cara shook her hair out—a terrible habit—and walked back over to him. 'Thank you for learning how to dance for my wedding,' she said with a grin. 'But promise me you won't keep mumbling the steps tomorrow night as you do them.'

'I was?' he asked in a shocked voice.

'You were—' she laughed '—just be glad I don't have video evidence!'

She gave a casual wave and walked out of the ballroom, leaving Arturo alone.

Alone to contemplate what she'd just said.

CHAPTER TWELVE

ROSA, THE MAID, was a dream. She'd come in with a tray of food as Darcy was unpacking her clothes. She'd taken one look at her outfit for the wedding tomorrow, which hadn't travelled quite as well as she'd hoped, and asked if she'd like Rosa to steam it for her.

She'd then directed Darcy to a walk-in cupboard where a few items were already hanging in covered sleeves.

'Mr Fabiano asked that some items were delivered for you for tonight. I believe he forgot to mention the family dinner.' Her eyes gleamed with amusement.

'He did,' said Darcy, staring at the items on the hangers, not sure if she liked Arturo buying clothes for her.

'Don't worry,' said Rosa conspiratorially. 'He has good taste, and said to pick whatever you like.' She turned to leave, but paused at the door. 'And if you don't like anything, come and find me. I'll be able to find you something to wear.'

She gave a wave and left the room.

How nice. Darcy's stomach growled, but she was too enticed now by the clothes in the walk-in closet. Her own things hanging there felt meagre in comparison, even though she was perfectly happy with them.

She unzipped the covers over the new clothes. The first was an elegant black jumpsuit with a black sequinned belt, the second a red dress by a popular Italian designer with matching red-soled shoes, the third another dress, this time in silver, with fine straps and a cowl neckline, and the last was a rose-pink dress with a square neck and ruched design that fell just below her knees.

All of these were gorgeous. She hesitated for around five seconds, then sent photos of them all to Fizz. As she sat down to eat, her table turned towards the display of clothes, Fizz gave her detailed thoughts on every dress. And whilst all of them were complimentary, they made her laugh out loud. It was almost as if her sister was in the room with her.

As she nibbled at the crusty bread, thin cut meat, cheese and olives she'd been brought, she walked into the grand bathroom and started running the shower. The truth was, she actually wanted to try all the outfits on. There was none she wanted to instantly dismiss. And that surprised her. Her initial indignation about Arturo buying her clothes had vanished. Granted, none of these clothes had price tags on them, and maybe if they did the indignation would return.

But, for now, she was just going to accept the gift with good grace. After all, if he'd warned her about a family dinner she would have brought something appropriate.

One hour later, showered, hair dried and make-up on, she stood in front of the full-length mirror admiring the black jumpsuit. She honestly liked it best, and when Rosa came back in the room with her crease-free dress for tomorrow she gave her an appreciative look.

'That's gorgeous. Is that the one you're going with?'

Darcy took one last look. The silver sandals matched impeccably and the black sequinned belt cinched the jumpsuit perfectly at her waist. 'It's the one I like best.'

'You look great.' Rosa hung up the dress Fizz had sent for her. 'As for tomorrow, your dress will look fantastic. What colour of wrist corsage would you like?'

'I think cream would be best.'

'No problem.'

There was a knock at the door, even though it was open, and she looked up to see Arturo standing in black trousers and a white shirt. He wore no tie, his dress shirt open at the neck and his jacket draped casually over his arm.

He walked in, not hiding the smile on his face at her choice of clothes. 'You look gorgeous.' He kissed her cheek and she gave a nervous laugh as Rosa was watching them.

He held out his arm for her and she joined him, walking down the curved staircase as he guided her to a room she'd only seen at a glance on the tour with Cara. His phone pinged and he pulled it from his pocket and silenced it without a word.

Some of the guests were already seated and she patiently let Arturo lead her around the room and introduce her to a host of aunts and uncles whose names she tried her best to remember.

As she settled in the chair next to him, a distinct feeling of unrest came over her. It wasn't the people, or the place. It was the wedding, and all the festivities around it, that were taking root in her brain and sparking memories she'd long since forgotten.

There was a round of applause and Dante and Cara entered, hand in hand, Dante in a smart suit and Cara in a spectacular green dress. Cara air kissed her way around the table, leaving no lipstick marks, her perfect smile never leaving her face. Instead of sitting at one end of the table, they sat together in the middle, giving themselves more opportunity to talk to their guests on either side.

'Cara looks beautiful,' Darcy murmured.

Arturo leaned a little closer. 'It's an Italian tradition. The bride wears green to the rehearsal dinner because it's supposed to bring good fortune for the happy couple's big day.'

'I hadn't thought about Italian traditions,' said Darcy softly, little pieces of panic taking seed in her brain.

Arturo didn't seem to notice. 'We have a few. I'll fill you in tomorrow.'

As drinks were served and food put in front of them, her skin prickled. She'd had a rehearsal dinner the night before her own wedding, with some of her relatives and Damian.

Hindsight was a wonderful thing, and whereas she'd thought him a bit jittery at the time, she hadn't paid attention to that. Laura had had a bad day at chemo a few days before and had tried her best to come for dinner, but lasted only a few minutes before going to lie down. The truth was, Darcy had been much more worried about her sister than any potential issues with her groom.

On reflection, Damian must have been feeling terrible. He'd drunk too much, not paid attention to the conversation around him and missed several jokes, clearly because he was thinking about other things. He'd asked to chat later, but Darcy had forgotten. Mainly because she'd been sitting at Laura's bedside, stroking her hair, as she wondered about the dark circles under Laura's eyes and the translucent appearance of her skin.

All of these things she'd pushed away. They'd been forgotten under the weight of actually being stood up at the altar. Warning signs she should have seen.

Warning signs that hadn't appeared in her brain much before now.

She'd been honest with Arturo and told him she hadn't attended a wedding since the disaster of her own. But somehow she'd totally underestimated how being here would make her feel. In truth, she hadn't expected it. And she hated the part of her brain that was allowing herself to dwell on the past, rather than focus on the present with this vivacious family and her gorgeous partner.

'You okay?' asked Arturo as she pushed her wine away.

'I'm fine,' she said automatically. 'Just decided to switch to water for now.'

He gave her an odd look, and she wondered if she'd just committed some cardinal sin by pushing Italian wine away whilst she was eating Italian food. But her stomach just couldn't cope.

The waiter filled her glass with water and she sipped as she nibbled at her food. It was delicious but her appetite had left her. A million things were catapulting around her brain, and she honestly couldn't believe she was being triggered by things five years on.

Even to her, it felt ridiculous. She'd reflected. She was adult enough to know it had been for the best. Yes, it had been upsetting at the time, but she'd got over it.

She wasn't even sure how much she'd actually loved Damian. She'd thought she had, but now wondered if it would ever have gone the distance.

'Something wrong with your food?' Arturo asked.

She put her hand on her abdomen. 'Nervous stomach,' she admitted. It wasn't a lie. It just wasn't entirely the truth either.

Many of the conversations around her were in Italian, and she was kicking herself for not trying to pick up a few basic words. She hadn't done languages at school for exams, so only knew a few sentences in French and Spanish, as those had been the basics they'd covered in the first year of high school.

Of course she'd only known Arturo for a few weeks, and he'd only asked her to the wedding barely one week ago, but if she'd forward planned she would have asked him for a few hints. Too late now.

It made her feel quite ignorant, and awkward. A wave came over her. On the way here she'd been slightly nervous. But sitting here now she felt completely and utterly out of her depth.

She was in a strange country, with lots of people speaking their own language, being triggered by just about everything around her in a way she could never have imagined for herself.

She could hear the almost silent buzz from Arturo's phone. It was clearly ringing out and he was still ignoring it. She could ask him about it, but she was too swamped with what else was happening.

She'd subconsciously noticed all the wedding preparations but hadn't let her focus go there. The beautiful flowers being brought in earlier today, the aroma in the household, the white linen and table settings visible in the marquee outside.

Arturo's hand closed over hers. 'Darcy?'

It was just the way he said her name. She

caught her breath, gave him a glance and said in a low voice, 'I need a moment.'

It must have been the look on her face. He stood up smoothly, but with no delay, and pulled her chair out for her.

She gave a brief smile and nod, muttering *Scusi* to those at the table, but didn't wait. She walked swiftly out the room, making a split-second decision. Did she want to be outside? Or somewhere inside?

Her legs made the decision for her, walking her quickly to the bathroom that Arturo had first shown her when they'd arrived at the house. She closed the door behind her with a click, then let herself slide down the cool tiled wall.

Black spots had entered her vision, but as soon as she reached the floor, her short sharp breathing started to slow.

She leaned forward, putting her head in her hands and concentrating on her breathing for a few moments, telling herself how ridiculous and pathetic this was.

She was a twenty-nine-year-old woman, and was sitting on some bathroom floor like a teenager. Shame flooded through her.

No. That wasn't helping. She lifted her head and leaned it back, letting the cold of the tile penetrate through to her scalp. Yes, that helped centre her a little.

Darcy closed her eyes, wishing she was miles away from this place right now and wouldn't have to make up some random excuse for her behaviour. She wasn't even sure how to explain what had just happened.

'Darcy?' The soft voice sounded at the door. 'Are you okay? Do you need me to get you anything?'

Darn it. Arturo. Of course it was. He was here for his sister's wedding. He should be concentrating on that. He should be enjoying himself.

This wasn't about her. *None* of this was about her. She took another few long breaths. Her mouth was so dry.

She pushed herself up from the floor, washed her hands first, then splashed some water on her face. Apart from the red spots high on her cheeks, she didn't look too bad.

She swallowed then clicked the door open. Arturo was pacing outside, worry evident across his face. He moved to her instantly. 'Is it all too much?'

She gulped, hating how she was feeling. 'I don't want to spoil the evening. Would you mind if I went to bed? I think I'm just over-tired.'

'If you can't do this—if it's all too much—you need to let me know.'

She swallowed, a huge lump in her throat at

how understanding he was being, and how truly pathetic she felt right now. 'I'm sorry. I'll be fine tomorrow,' and even as she said the words, her brain told her that she had to be. She had to get past this. She had to move on with her life.

He put his arm gently behind her and walked her up the stairs to her room, giving her a soft kiss on the cheek at the door. 'Do you want me to stay with you?'

It was the first time she didn't want to say yes. She needed to sort her head out. She needed to understand why she felt so swamped.

'I'll be fine. Go, join your family. But thank you. I'll see you in the morning.'

She could see the tiny shards of regret in his eyes, but couldn't let herself be influenced by them.

He gave her a nod as she closed the door. She waited a moment before moving over to her bed. In the quickest change known to man, she slipped off the beautiful jumpsuit and her underwear, and pulled on her dark green shortie pyjamas, only noticing the colour at the last minute.

She still needed some air, so moved to the large windows and pulled one open, sitting on the window seat, with her back against the frame and her bent leg poised at the edge.

As the cool Italian air drifted in, she felt instantly better. It carried with it the aroma of the wedding flowers but, instead of distressing her, now she was alone, she just closed her eyes and let her body cool down.

She could call Fizz. She could call Libby. She could tell either one of them what had just happened, and that right now she felt as if she couldn't trust herself, or her own judgement.

But how did you explain something you didn't really understand yourself?

Tears glistened in her eyes. She had to hold things together. She had to keep her emotions in check—but then Arturo's face came into her head.

How was it for him? She'd been so focused on herself she hadn't considered him. His family home must be throwing up memories for him too, likely of his father.

He had to step into his father's shoes tomorrow and give his sister away. The pressure was real. They'd laughed and joked at the dance class, but now she'd had a glimpse of his family life and estate, she understood why he'd wanted things to be perfect for his sister.

Embarrassment swept over her again. He needed support right now, not a girlfriend who was crumbling.

Girlfriend? Was that what she was? She didn't even know that. What she did know was that she was glad to have a little space right now to try and sort her head out.

Tomorrow was another day.

And she only hoped she could get through it.

CHAPTER THIRTEEN

HE HADN'T SLEPT well last night, which was never a good idea when the next day would be so full-on.

He'd had breakfast at five, then again at six, with Dante, who was a mixture of nervous and excited all rolled into one. He was actually a joy to be around, and Arturo was delighted that he would be a full-time family member.

Cara had warned Arturo away from 'her half of the house' this morning. He hadn't even had the energy to laugh at her last night, and just agreed that he would pick her up at the last moment, to escort her down the stairs and out for the wedding. He could only imagine the chaos going on in those rooms today.

But even though today was all about his sister, the person whose room he was most curious about was Darcy.

She'd revealed part of herself before they came, and he accepted she might find some moments difficult. But other thoughts were circling in his head. If, five years on, weddings still affected her like this, was she really ready to move on? And if she wasn't ready—five years after the fact—would she ever be?

It wasn't the kind of conversation he wanted to have with her. Because then he would need to let her know that his feelings were developing into something so much stronger than he'd ever predicted. He'd seen her eyes yesterday when she'd taken in the vastness of the property. He didn't have a single worry that Darcy would be interested in his money, inheritance or family estate. The truth was, she'd looked downright terrified.

He moved across his room and touched the picture on his desk. It was from years before, him and his father together at a family ball, both in short-sleeved shirts and both laughing with their arms around each other. It hurt him with an ache he didn't like to acknowledge.

He brushed his finger across the glass. 'I'll do you proud today, Papà,' he said softly, then paused for a moment. 'I wish you could have met her. I brought her here, and now I wonder if I did the right thing.' He took a breath and looked out over the countryside stretching before him.

What he'd learned last night from his mother,

and what he had to do today, had given him an insight into his current life he hadn't seen before. He had to take that into account today. Particularly when he'd finally answered the person last night who'd been desperate to get hold of him, and that conversation had been littered with innuendo and unspoken threats. He didn't take kindly to that kind of talk, and his phone was now in his bedside cabinet until this wedding was over.

The threats had never meant much to him. Since the death of Faye, and of his father, he hadn't really considered what might happen if someone decided to see a threat through. His mother and Cara would be taken care of. If he wasn't around any more, apart from his direct family, who would actually care?

The thought made him shudder. For the first time in five years, he considered someone other than his direct family—Darcy. It was like a little flower bud opening inside his brain. A chance again. A real chance at life. Perhaps the chance of love again? As the petals unfurled, he knew he had so much to consider. Maybe now was the time to reevaluate his future.

He knew today he had to concentrate on Cara. But once the wedding was over, he would be heading back to Edinburgh with Darcy.

That made a warm feeling spread through him. He had to let her know that it was time to move their relationship on. Time to see where things could take them.

He only hoped that she would agree.

CHAPTER FOURTEEN

ROSA BROUGHT BREAKFAST to her room, and helped her fasten the tiny buttons on the back of her dress.

She turned around to get a good look in the full-length mirror. The lime-green satin dress was stunning, and was certainly something she wouldn't have picked herself.

It reached the floor but had a spectacular split, revealing some leg. It had tiny straps and a cowl neckline—similar to the silver dress that Arturo had picked for her. Maybe she should wear that, maybe the lime-green was too daring.

She held out her arm as Rosa fastened the corsage to her wrist. 'Maybe I should change? This dress is very fitted. It might be too much for a wedding.'

'Don't you dare,' scolded Rosa. 'You look fantastic, and remember I've seen some of the other guests. It's going to be a multitude of colours down there.' She looked up and down the length of Darcy. 'And while your dress is figure-hugging, there's nothing on show.' She winked. 'Just a bit of leg, and who doesn't like that?'

Darcy started to laugh. Rosa had been so nice since she'd arrived yesterday. She bit her lip and asked a nervous question. 'Is Arturo okay this morning? And the rest of the family?'

Rosa darted a glance at her. 'Arturo ate three breakfasts this morning. I don't know if it was nerves, or if he was covering every sitting to see if you would come down.' She looked at Darcy's wide eyes and shook her head. 'He's fine, as is Cara. In fact, I've been out of her range for nearly fifteen minutes. She'll have a list for me by now.'

Darcy took a few nervous steps. 'When should I go down?'

She could see other guests had arrived and were mixing in the garden. But since she didn't really know anyone and Arturo would clearly be with his sister, she didn't want to get in anyone's way.

'Give it another fifteen minutes,' advised Rosa, 'then go on down.' She disappeared out of the door.

Darcy moved to stand at the window. She wanted to focus on Arturo, and how he might be feeling today. She didn't want to think about herself in any way. That just seemed selfish. Today was Cara and Dante's wedding. They deserved the best day. And she would make sure that nothing she said or did would get in the way of that.

Thirty minutes later, the guests were still waiting. Dante looked handsome in his well-cut suit, his brother next to him. Their feet were starting to shuffle as they kept glancing towards the door of the house as they stood under the pink and white rose arch.

The man next to her had quickly realised she was English and had spoken to her a few times. He glanced at his watch. 'My bet was on thirty minutes, so I'm hoping she appears now.'

Darcy blinked. 'You bet on how late the bride would be?'

'You didn't?' He looked surprised. 'Of course, you're Arturo's new girlfriend. You wouldn't have known about this.' He glanced around at the other guests occupying the white linen-backed chairs in the Italian sun. 'I think around fifty per cent of the guests put a bet on Cara being late.'

Darcy's mouth fell open, and he leaned forward and whispered, 'Remember, we're mainly family. We know this girl.'

There was some rustling, and the celebrant

clapped their hands, bringing the guests to attention. The music started, and Darcy felt a little bit sick.

She turned her head and watched as Arturo and Cara walked down the aisle together. Cara's dress was beautiful, the top Italian lace with a white underlay, but her skin showing across her neckline and down her arms. The skirt was full, and she had a long veil that trailed magnificently behind her.

Arturo was wearing an immaculate dark suit, the same as Dante and his brother's. His bow tie and bright white shirt made his skin seem more tanned than usual. He caught her eye, and she saw the hint of a smile at the corners of his lips.

Then she turned back. It was an unexpected moment. If she'd thought things through last night, she might have pre-planned not to catch this second.

The second that Dante caught sight of his bride. There it was. The look on his face of pure and utter joy at seeing the woman he loved arrive for their wedding.

It was like a vice of steel clamping around her heart. Because she'd never had this moment. Her groom hadn't appeared.

Her breath caught in her throat as she blinked back some unexpected tears. She forced herself to turn back to look at Cara. The look was mirrored on Cara's face. She was overjoyed to be walking towards her groom. The love between these two was there for everyone to see.

The vice started to release on Darcy's heart, the gut-punch relieving itself from her clenched stomach.

Damian would never have looked like that at her, and she would never have looked like that at him.

She'd always known that the breakup had been for the best. But even though she'd told herself that all these years, she hadn't really faced up to what it meant.

It meant that she hadn't been paying attention to her relationship. She'd allowed things to drift on when they weren't right. She'd allowed herself to plan a wedding with the biggest thought in her head being that she wanted her sister still to be there for her wedding.

Her legs were momentarily like jelly and she gripped the back of the seat in front of her. The celebrant had started to talk, and the groom had presented the bride with her bouquet—another Italian tradition she hadn't known about.

There was such tenderness in the look between the bride and groom, and Darcy felt a pang in her heart. She wanted that. She wanted that moment between her and the man that she loved. She wanted someone to look at her the way Dante was currently looking at Cara.

A breeze blew across her skin and she remembered the occasions when Arturo had looked at her like that. A number of times when she couldn't wipe the smile off her face when she was in his company. The sensation of his lips on hers. His skin against hers.

The recognition made her catch her breath. Could he have looked at her that way because he loved her?

Her legs felt a bit weak as she recognised her strength of feeling towards him. They'd been tiptoeing around the edges. Probably because things had moved so fast. But she'd never felt like this about someone. Never felt a connection like she currently did with him. Even the thought of Arturo filled her whole body with a warm glow. The glow of love. Her smile spread further. Should she be scared right now? Should she be panicking because she'd known him such a short space of time?

But she wasn't. She didn't feel like that at all. What she did know for sure was that she couldn't wait for him to be by her side again. Hand in hand, lips together. For the first time in a very long time everything felt just right.

Then other thoughts crowded her brain. He had family. He had family in Italy, and very clearly a place here. For now, in Edinburgh, Arturo seemed a bit rootless. He'd brought her here as 'protection' against his family. Maybe she was reading this all wrong. Maybe he didn't feel the same way about her at all. This guy had a dangerous job that he'd warned her about. If she continued a relationship with him, could she be putting herself in danger?

The seesawing of her emotions made her feel giddy. From one extreme to the other in virtually a few seconds. How could she trust herself right now?

Arturo shook hands with Dante and kissed his sister on the cheek. As he moved back to sit in the front row with his mother, his brown eyes met Darcy's, swiftly running up and down her body, then he winked at her and mouthed the word, 'Wow'.

And with that single word, her world catapulted yet again. Into a place where she might consider a future at his side.

Laura's face flashed into her brain, and for the first time ever she took a breath and pushed it away. Today was about celebrating a gorgeous couple's wedding.

And as her face tilted into a smile for Arturo she let herself focus on only one thing—the here and now.

CHAPTER FIFTEEN

THE WEDDING WENT BEAUTIFULLY. Darcy—although not one of the immediate family—had sat by his side during the meal. He'd noticed a few eyes on them throughout the proceedings, and could tell that his more eager relatives were waiting to pounce and ask questions.

Cara hadn't quite been prepared for his father of the bride speech. He'd joked to her about it on several occasions. But when he'd broken it to his friends and family that his father had already written his father of the bride speech for Cara a few years before, silence had filled the room.

Those in the family knew why his father had done that. His mother's head was bowed, even though she'd been the person who had told Arturo. His father had written his speech when his life had been threatened ten years earlier over an artefact. He'd taken things *that* seriously.

And the impact that had on Arturo couldn't be underestimated.

It hadn't mattered that he'd known that his father's death had not been related to his work in any form. What mattered was that for a time his father had believed the threat to be real. And in accordance with that he'd taken some steps, one of which was writing his father of the bride speech for Cara's potential future wedding.

Arturo held Cara's hand as he said his father's words, his voice cracking in places. They'd only needed to be amended a little. Then he added some gracious words about Dante and what a wonderful addition to the family he would be.

By the time he finished the room erupted with applause. Cara's make-up was a mess and he might get into trouble at a later date, but the bear hug she'd given him let him know he'd be entirely forgiven.

As he looked next to him at Darcy in her stunning green dress, he could see tears flowing freely down her face and she looked as though she might be shaking.

He wanted to hug her too. But he had to support his sister first and foremost. So, in front of his family and friends, he reached down, took Darcy's hand and put it to his chest. It was a momentary gesture. And he was surprised by how many eyebrows raised at the intimacy of it.

Darcy blinked, leaving her hand on his chest, and blew him a little kiss with her other hand, the barest and most exposed of smiles on her face. And in that moment he knew. He knew that he loved her.

It had been there at the edges of his mind for the last few days. It didn't matter that it hadn't even been a month since they'd met. He'd never felt like this. Not with Faye. Not with anyone. Everything about this relationship had been out of step from the beginning. Their odd meeting. The bucket list. The fact he'd invited someone he'd only known for a short while to the most important family wedding he would ever attend. Deep down, he knew. He knew he had to ask her, because this just felt right. There were no other words for it. Darcy was the person he wanted to be with—despite all the other things he had to sort out—and he only hoped she might feel the same way.

The meal was finished, the toasts were made, and before they moved onto the evening reception, Dante and Cara broke the traditional glass, which shattered into a million pieces— the pieces signifying how many years they would have together.

The wedding guests cheered and raised their glasses in another toast.

As they moved from the marquee to the ballroom for the dancing, Arturo was caught with two elderly aunts for a few moments and bombarded with questions about Darcy, which he didn't completely answer. Once he saw them to their seats, he scanned the crowd for the lime-green dress. She should be easy to spot. But she wasn't.

He weaved his way through his family and friends, being stopped every few steps. It was difficult. Most of them wanted to talk about his father, and some, of course, about the potential of a 'new' family member. He couldn't walk away, even though the more the conversations grew, so did the lump in his throat.

Before he knew it, Cara was at his side, her face now immaculate once again. 'It's time to dance, dear brother,' she said.

He gave one last scan of the crowd for Darcy again. But he couldn't spot her, then accompanied his sister back to where his mother and Dante stood.

He knew the instructions for this part. Dante and Cara would dance first, followed by Arturo dancing with his sister, while Dante danced with his mother-in-law. After that, he would likely dance with a few more members of the wedding party, before hopefully, finding Darcy once again.

The first dance went like a dream. He could bet that Dante and Cara had also taken lessons, because their dance was smooth and elegant, followed by a little bit of fun funk at the end. He sent a silent prayer upwards that Cara wouldn't try anything impromptu like that with him.

On the music cue, he moved into place beside his sister, with a little bow of his head, before moving into position. As the Viennese waltz began he counted very loudly—in his head. But as they continued, he didn't need to count. It seemed that some of the things Margaret had told him were finally clicking into place. It became easier and smoother to dance, it felt more natural. Even with the layers of Cara's dress, it didn't throw him off balance, or accidentally step on her toes. And when they finally finished to a rousing applause, he was happy, relieved, and couldn't stop smiling.

He caught a glimpse of green. Darcy gave him a wide smile and a thumbs-up. As tradition dictated, the next dance was with his mother. By the time it was finished, he had only one thought on his mind.

He moved through the ballroom, then the bar area and the quieter room where some people were sitting, before finally making his way outside to the garden terrace. Darcy's silhouette was clear, her dress stunning. And as he walked up behind her, he could see the goosepimples on her flesh.

He slipped off his jacket and put it around her shoulders. She gave a little jolt, glanced over her shoulder, then shot him a wide smile as she pulled the jacket around her body.

'What are you doing out here?'

'Just contemplating the world,' she said in a faraway tone. 'It's been a beautiful day.'

He bent down and kissed the side of her neck. 'Since the meal, I've hardly seen you. I'm so sorry.'

'No, it's fine,' she said. 'There's been plenty to keep me occupied.'

'Please tell me you haven't been bombarded by my relatives.'

She held up one hand and counted on her fingers. 'Who am I? How old am I? Do we live together? Are we engaged? How long have we known each other? Can I cook? Do I like children? When am I moving to Italy?' She sighed and let her head hang down for a second.

'Oh, Darcy, I'm so sorry. If it's any help, I've had exactly the same questions.'

She hugged the jacket around her body. 'Let's

just say, Italian families are…interesting,' she finished.

She spun around and wrapped her arms around his waist, leaning her head against his shoulder.

He was almost scared to ask. 'Are you okay?'

She looked back up at him and he could swear he saw something flicker behind her eyes. 'I am,' she said. 'When we get back to Edinburgh, we need to have a chat.'

It was like a stone settling in his stomach. He couldn't argue, because he knew he needed to be honest with her—about how he was feeling. He wanted to be, because he wanted, more than anything, to give this relationship a chance.

His mother hadn't presented him with the father of the bride speech until last night. She hadn't found it before then. It had been in an envelope tucked next to the diamond necklace that they'd always agreed would be Cara's on her wedding day. His mother hadn't had any reason to open the velvet jewellery case before then.

Darcy threaded her hands through his hair. 'How about I get a dance? I hate to think I've put in all these hours of practise with you, and then don't even dance with you on the day.' She had a soft smile on her face, but he could see an edge of sadness in it. Or was he imagining it? Was this a farewell dance? He couldn't find the words to ask.

'Of course,' he agreed, his mouth dry as he took her hand in his and led her to the ballroom dance floor.

As they took their positions he leaned forward and whispered in her ear, 'Have I told you how fantastic you look today?'

She gave a smile, which reached right up into her eyes. 'Not too shocking?'

'Not shocking at all,' he replied, his voice low and husky. 'Just entirely sexy.'

She laughed. 'I'll let Fizz know that you approve.'

The music had started and he spun her around. He didn't need to count this time. Dancing with Darcy had no pressure around it. They moved as one. After weeks of practice, it was as if they were meant to be in this position.

Due to the design of her dress, his hands were on bare skin at one point, and satin at the other. Although they both knew the frame and position Margaret had taught them, they were more relaxed and closer than normal.

It seemed easier that way. There were no missteps. No wrong timing. The music wasn't ideal for the Viennese waltz but neither of them seemed to notice, and as the music drew to a close, Arturo did one final spin, then bent Darcy backwards in a surprise move that they'd both seen professional dancers do.

She let her back arch and leg extend as he did it, and instead of a look of surprise she greeted him with a wide smile. Even whilst she was back in this position she whispered, 'Isn't this where you're supposed to kiss me?'

He supported her back and touched his lips to hers, gradually pulling her upwards as he did so.

Her arms changed position and entwined around his neck. Her body pressed against his as they both were fully upright. An elderly aunt and uncle next to them on the dance floor made some encouraging comments and Arturo let his lips reluctantly part from Darcy's to acknowledge them. She started to laugh. He bent his head so their foreheads rested together.

'Still can't speak Italian,' she murmured. 'Was it approval or disapproval?'

'I think we can safely say it was approval,' he replied with a smile on his face.

He felt her draw in a deep breath. 'Have you done all your duties this evening?' she asked.

'I hope so,' he said, sweeping a glance across the dance floor. 'I've done everything on the very long list that Cara sent me, except one.'

She tilted her head. 'What's the last one?'

'It's around the final dance at a wedding. Commonly known as La Tarantella. And it's usually guaranteed to make guests dizzy.'

She looked the tiniest bit sad. 'Then I guess we'd better wait.'

His heart clenched, and he absolutely wanted to ditch his sister's wedding at this point and just take Darcy upstairs. He wondered if Cara would even miss them. But a wave of responsibility swept over him. Of course she would miss them, and would likely be disappointed. If he knew Cara at all, she would spend the rest of her life telling him he'd missed the last dance at her wedding.

So he tightened his grip on Darcy's hand, got them both some cocktails and took a comfortable seat and introduced her to some more family members.

He could see her concentrating hard, listening to the variety of accents. Most of his family spoke English well, a few stumbled over sentences, and after a while she turned to him, almost embarrassed. 'I should have made more of an effort. I should have learned some Italian before we came.'

He looked at her in surprise, because it had never even entered his mind. 'You hardly had the time. It's a nice thought though.' He swallowed before adding, 'Maybe next time.'

But his brain was whirring. Would he bring her back here? Would she want to come back, after he told her how he felt about her?

Things were taking on an entirely different perspective for Arturo now. Threats in the past he'd treated with disdain. Arturo was able enough to deal with anyone who decided to get physical. But he hadn't realised what kind of threats might have been made against his mother or sister in the past. Arturo didn't have a family—yet. Would he want to expose his future potential family to possible threats? Of course not.

His blood ran cold. Because there was only one person in his head right now. Darcy. And deep down to his core, he knew how he would react if anyone threatened her.

He'd known her for three weeks. If this was how he felt after three weeks, how would he feel in three months, three years, or three decades?

And how did he even start a conversation like that?

He ran his hand through his dark hair. These were his issues. All his. He had to deal with them, because the last thing he wanted was any consequences for the woman next to him.

She was talking again to his aunt. Her eyes were bright, her blonde hair shining, and her skin glowed under the soft lights in the room. She really was the most beautiful woman he'd ever seen. Without even thinking, he ran his finger down her arm and, without hesitation, she let his hand reach hers and threaded their fingers together.

The music changed and there was a variety of shouting. 'Time to join the final dance.' He smiled at her.

'Show me what to do,' she said simply.

The guests formed a circle around the bride and groom, joining hands together. There were too many for one circle, so some guests also formed an outer circle. The music started, the tempo quick and increasing with every beat. The guests began to rotate clockwise as the music speeded up, the circle on the outside going anticlockwise. At one point, there was chaos as people came to a halt, then started to go in the reverse direction.

It didn't take long for Darcy to get the hang of things. She even kicked off her shoes as she stumbled a few times. The music reached a frenzied pitch as the guests shouted good wishes to the bride and groom in the middle of the circles and everyone almost collapsed in a heap at the crescendo of the music.

Arturo dropped hands and turned to pick up

Darcy by the waist, spinning her around and kissing her on the lips as he set her back down.

'Can we lie down now?' she asked, looking up at him with those pale blue eyes.

He took her hand and led her through the crowd, still celebrating and coming down from the last dance. They made their way upstairs and along to Arturo's room.

Darcy leaned back against the door as it closed behind them, glanced downwards and flicked the lock.

He pulled off his tie, which was already loose around his neck, as she walked slowly towards him, before spinning around to show him the back of her dress.

'I think I'm going to need a little help with this,' she murmured over her shoulder in a low, husky voice.

He stared at the array of tiny buttons, wanting to wrench them apart, but instead taking his time to slowly, meticulously undo them one by one.

He got distracted, kissing her shoulders then her back as he released one after the other, before finally letting the thin straps drop down from her shoulders as she turned back around.

Her fingers were quicker than his, undoing the buttons on his shirt and trousers before her own dress dropped to the ground.

'You're sure?' he asked.

'Oh, I'm sure,' she breathed in response.

He walked her backwards to the bed and laughed as they fell on top of it.

And all talking stopped.

CHAPTER SIXTEEN

IT WAS FUNNY how some parts of her life seemed to move in slow motion, and others at break-neck speed.

After the perfect night in Arturo's bed, there hadn't been time for the chat they both knew they needed to have. Their flight was that day, and after she'd gone back to her own rooms to pack and had breakfast it was time to leave.

Cara, Dante and Arturo's mother had been gracious. If they'd noticed anything, or the change in sleeping arrangements, they were too polite to mention it.

From the moment they'd taken off from the airport, Darcy had found herself overtaken with tiredness and had slept most of the flight home. Arturo had wakened her with a smile, whilst she'd been leaning against him as the plane moved to descend.

He dropped her home with a kiss on the lips but made no indication he wanted to come in.

She wasn't quite sure what to tell either Fizz or Libby. So she messaged both with a few photos to say the wedding was wonderful, but not giving any indication of what had happened between her and Arturo. She knew she should have a conversation with one or both of them about how unexpectedly triggering she'd found the wedding, and the host of other emotions that had swept over her. But she just couldn't go there.

Instead, she focused on the bucket list. Because that was what had got her here.

The first two tasks had led to her attending the wedding. It had led to her facing up to part of the reason she'd built walls around herself, and also prompted her to examine why she hadn't felt able to start another relationship where she could invest herself totally.

Could Laura really have imagined any of this happening? Or had the message from Laura just given her the push to look at herself and the world around her in a different way?

She stared at number three on the list.

Make a lifetime commitment to something or someone.

She could remember the look on Arturo's face when she'd mentioned this one, and the fleeting glance had made her think that maybe—just maybe—he might have feelings developing for her, the way she had for him.

But Darcy didn't want to push. She didn't want Arturo to feel as if she was angling for more than he was willing to give. Their increased closeness gave her hope, but she wasn't naïve enough to think any further than that.

Instead, she needed to focus on herself. Making a commitment for the last few years *had* been tough on her—even though she hadn't recognised it at the time.

Signing her various work contracts had made her edgy. Signing for a mortgage on this beautiful property had actually made her feel quite sick, even though she loved it and the further renovations had worked out perfectly.

Now—a further commitment. What could that mean for her?

But there, at the back of her mind, was something. Something that had been nagging away at her, drifting into her head when she watched mindless TV, read a book that didn't completely capture her attention, or was just in that little spot between almost sleep and total sleep.

Could she really do something like this? She opened the browser on her computer—because the page had been bookmarked. Then she picked up the phone and dialled.

* * *

Arturo was furious with himself. He'd made contact again with the business associate who had been trying to warn him off an artefact. The bottom line was it had been stolen. And even though the current owners hadn't been the guilty party, they were still reluctant to relinquish their prize.

Arturo had been involved in many of these 'debates' over the years. Some people would prefer things were kept in dark cellars or basements than be allowed to be admired or enjoyed in a museum. Even when families didn't know they actually owned something, then discovered it through the gift of inheritance, they were still strangely reluctant to give up something that wasn't theirs to have. People had strange ideas about ownership. They had even stranger ideas about provenance.

He'd had a breakneck trip to Berlin. Then another to Sicily. He'd then received a phone call with a more explicit threat. And his mind had focused more completely than ever.

But Darcy had messaged and asked him if he would go somewhere today. She hadn't said where, but his response had been immediate. He would follow her just about anywhere these days, and he really, really wanted to sit down and talk to her.

As he pulled up outside her house, he noticed there was a different car parked outside. This one was a large four-by-four. Did she have another visitor?

She opened her door as he exited the car and gave him a broad smile. 'Like my new wheels? We'll have to take mine, as yours won't suit.'

He glanced at his low-slung sports car. There were a number of places it might not suit, so he smiled and climbed into the passenger seat of her new car.

'Mystery,' he said slowly. 'I think I like it, but where are we going?'

She gave him a smile, then took a slow breath. 'Since you've helped me with the first two things on my bucket list, I thought I'd invite you along to help with the third.'

His stomach squirmed. The commitment one. More or less what he wanted to talk to her about. He just didn't know where this one was going to go. But he had to be absolutely upfront with her before he could expect her to know whether she would consider a relationship with him.

'Where are we going?' he asked, not sure what the answer would be.

'Just watch and wait,' she said then tapped his leg. 'I think you'll be surprised.'

As they started along the road, he decided it

was time to tackle the situation that had been on his mind since the wedding. Truthfully, it had probably been even longer than that.

'Do we have time to stop somewhere for coffee, or an early lunch? Just to have a chance to talk.'

She shot him a sideways glance. 'No,' she said, and it seemed like an honest answer, which made him wonder if she was avoiding the topic of any kind of relationship between them. 'I've got a set time I need to be at the… this place.'

He frowned and she gave him a soft smile. 'Be patient. I'm a bit nervous about this one.'

He shot her a glance and she quickly added, 'I'm quite indecisive sometimes.'

'You are? Can't say I've noticed that about you,' he mentioned. 'But I have to warn you, I can be…what's that word Scots people use… crabbit, if I haven't had coffee.'

She laughed. 'Me too. But I promise we're going to endorphin city right now. Just be patient.'

Fifteen minutes later they pulled up in front of the last place he would have expected. 'Ready?' she asked.

'Not at all,' he said as they climbed out of the car.

The rescue centre was immaculate, and they

were met at the reception desk by a woman named Jen, who shook Darcy's hand warmly.

'Hi Darcy. As you know from the email I sent, everything went very well with the home check. Probably because you'd already put a lot of safeguards in place. Now, it's time for me to find you the perfect match.' She held up one hand. 'But don't be disappointed if you don't find someone today. Sometimes it takes a few visits to find the perfect match.'

She looked over at Arturo, and Darcy quickly said, 'Jen, this is my friend Arturo. I'm hoping he'll help me choose.'

The noise of some dogs barking was clearly heard from the reception area, and they were led through the back to a whole row of inside kennels for the dogs in the rescue centre. Jen took them over to the nearest to show them a label. 'So, each dog has some information available. Their name, age, breed if we know it, and some key facts about what kind of home would be best for them. It mentions if they can be housed with other dogs or cats, if children can be in the home. It also mentions any special conditions required for the dog, or any known issues. We are scrupulously honest because we want to find the perfect home for them all. One of the worst things we can do is send a dog to a potential home then have them returned because the new owner had unrealistic expectations.'

Darcy nodded solemnly. 'I understand.' She took a deep breath, but she couldn't help but smile. 'I'm ready.'

Jen gave a nod. 'Take your time. If you want to spend some time with a particular dog, let me know and I'll open the kennel and take you through to our meeting room.' She gave a final serious smile. 'Come and find me when you're ready.' Then she walked down to an office and left them to it.

'You're adopting a dog?' Arturo was still a bit stunned.

'I'm adopting a dog,' she repeated, her smile widening. 'I've had my home assessment. I've talked to the farmer next door, and he's repaired the hole in his fence. I've bought some basics, and the rest I'll get once I know for sure who picks me.'

'Who picks you?'

She licked her lips nervously. 'Apparently, my friends who already have dogs have told me that really, they pick you, instead of you picking them.'

'I'm going to pretend that makes sense,' said Arturo.

They started to walk along the row of kennels. Some of the dogs were inquisitive and came to meet them. Some of the dogs ignored them. Some barked or yapped. A few growled. But Darcy stopped at every kennel, read the card and bent down to see the dog.

After a few minutes, Arturo seemed to warm up, and got down to look at the dogs too. 'How long have you been considering this?' he asked. There was tension in the way he asked the question.

'Since we met that woman on the beach. It just made sense to me.'

They'd finished the length of the room and walked back down the other side. Some of the dogs were puppies, full of life and energy, others were clearly a bit older and more relaxed. She was glad of the identity cards since some of the breeds were unfamiliar to her.

'So, what size of dog do you want?' asked Arturo. 'Have you decided that much?' He was down on his knees, a Yorkshire terrier licking his fingers through the bars.

She laughed. 'I don't really have a preference. My house and land are big enough for any size of dog.'

She kept wandering along, stopping to talk to every dog, but eventually standing up and stretching her back.

Arturo came up beside her. 'No one pick you yet?'

She pressed her lips together and thought for a few moments. 'No, but I have an idea.'

She walked along to Jen's open office and stood in the doorway. Jen stood up, keys on her belt ready. 'Is there someone you'd like to meet?'

Darcy took a breath. 'Actually, I want you to help me. Show me the dog that no one else wants—the one that no one considers.'

Jen gave her a strange look, then bent her head. She was clearly thinking about something. After a few moments, she looked straight at Darcy, her eyes deadly serious.

She cleared her throat. 'I have an older dog. An absolute beauty. She's a former service dog.'

Arturo frowned. 'She sounds wonderful. Why does no one want her?'

Jen gave them both a nod to follow her and started down another corridor. 'Ruby is older. She's a red Lab. Labradors can be prone to joint problems. She has hip dysplasia. She had one hip replacement a few years ago, but is considered a risk for further anaesthetic.' Jen sighed and turned to face them both. It was clear she wanted to lay her cards on the table. 'Most people don't want to adopt a dog later in life, with complex health and care needs. She'll be impossible to insure, and her hydrotherapy costs eight hundred pounds a month alone. Your average person just doesn't have the finances to cover that.'

'I do.' The words were out of Darcy's mouth straight away. She looked at the expression on Jen's face, and Arturo's, and put her hand on her chest. 'No, honestly, I do. I work in cyber-security. I've done well over the last few years. I can pay the expenses that will be needed. If Ruby likes me, of course.'

Jen seemed relieved. 'Okay,' she said and took them around a corner, where a red Labrador retriever lay on a comfortable bed. She had soft eyes and an adorable face. 'Hey Ruby,' said Jen, kneeling down beside her.

Ruby got to her feet. It wasn't quite a struggle. But it was clear she didn't weight bear evenly on all four paws. She still seemed good-natured and happy to be around people.

Darcy sat down next to her and talked to her. 'Hello Ruby. I'm here to see you today. You are the most handsome girl. What a beautiful colour. Everybody must just love you.' She rubbed Ruby's head, ears, and then started clapping her body as Ruby seemed to regard her carefully.

'So, you said Ruby was a service dog—what does that mean?' asked Arturo. 'Was she a guide dog?'

Jen shook her head, as she too clapped Ruby.

'No, nothing so simple. Ruby was trained to alert her owner to oncoming epileptic seizures. She was very good at her job. She would sense something and pull her owner's sleeve, letting her know to get down on the ground. Ruby would stay with her when she seized, watching over her and alerting assistance if required.'

'So, what happened?' Darcy asked.

Jen sighed. 'Her owner went to an event where the organisers didn't understand what a service dog was. They wouldn't let her enter. The owner went in, went to the toilet, had a seizure in the toilet area and fell and hit her head. Apparently, Ruby was going crazy outside and the staff called the police. They didn't even realise something had happened to the owner until the police entered to speak to her. Ruby was crying and whining. Her owner unfortunately died, and by then Ruby was too old to be matched as a service dog. She came to us instead, where we quickly realised she had joint issues. She's our longest resident. Three years.'

'Three years!' said Darcy, shocked that this beautiful dog hadn't managed to be rehomed. Ruby had lain down now and put her head on Darcy's lap. She was looking up at her with big brown eyes. Darcy leaned over and kissed her.

'Is this what it means when a dog chooses

you?' Arturo said softly, his face only inches away from hers.

'How old is she?' asked Darcy, since there was no immediate card for Ruby.

'She's ten,' said Jen. 'The average age of a Labrador is around twelve.'

Darcy nodded. Jen had known exactly what she was asking. Darcy bent down and put her face next to Ruby's. 'Ruby,' she said in a soft voice, 'how would you like to spend the rest of your days with me?'

Something held Arturo's heart firmly and clamped hard. Those words. They touched him in a way that he was certain they shouldn't.

His head was spinning. After their connection at the wedding, Darcy had looked at her bucket list and decided her commitment was to…a dog.

While at heart he knew it was a good and kind gesture, he had to ask himself why the commitment hadn't been to him. To them. Being here today was compounding exactly how he felt about her. He'd asked to speak to her, and she'd made an excuse. Rightly, he should have tried to talk to her over the last few days, but work had been hectic.

Work had also been clarifying. He'd made a decision, one he wanted to sit down and talk to Darcy about. Had he got things all wrong? Had their closeness at the wedding not meant anything at all?

Maybe he was misjudging things completely. In his head, he'd been considering things. If they had a real chance at a relationship, he'd wondered if Darcy would think about moving to Italy. He knew that would be a huge step, but since she was just about to adopt a dog that step would be off the cards for the next few years.

He didn't want to have that conversation here. But it was clear when she'd been planning her future she'd not been considering leaving Scotland.

Things moved quickly. Darcy signed paper-work and took a note of particular things for Ruby, like her hydrotherapy appointments, her treatment plan and medication, what food suited her and what her normal routine was. Darcy was enthusiastic about every part of this.

Jen gave her a lead and collar for Ruby, then bent down herself to pat and kiss the dog. It was clear she was very fond of Ruby. 'You take her for four hours today as a trial, bring her back, and we'll do the same thing a few times this week, until we make sure she's settled and happy.'

Darcy nodded. 'Absolutely. I'll do everything I need to do.'

'If all goes well, in around ten days, Ruby will be yours.'

Darcy couldn't wipe the smile off her face.

She pulled out some things that were already stowed in the boot of the car, including a harness and dog seat belt and a comfortable blanket for Ruby to settle on for the journey home.

As they waved and drove away, she turned in an unexpected direction. 'Where are we going?' asked Arturo.

'A few places,' said Darcy. 'We're going to take her down to the beach for a few minutes. Apparently, she used to love going to the beach. Then we need to stop at a pet store to pick up her food, and although I have a bed I think I need a bigger one. Then—' she gave him a big smile '—we'll go to the drive-through and pick up some coffee for us and a pup cup for Ruby.'

'A pup cup?'

'What? I've seen people do it online. Let's see if Ruby likes them.'

Arturo hated himself for feeling agitated by a dog. He glanced over his shoulder. She was a beauty, and he needed to get his thoughts into some kind of perspective. A dog. Something he'd never even thought about.

'Is Ruby going to be the most spoiled dog in the universe?'

'She's in her golden years,' said Darcy firmly. 'She deserves to be the happiest I can make her.'

An hour later, Ruby had paddled in the shallow waves with a little bounce in her step, they'd picked up her food and new bed, and she had shown them just how much she loved a pup cup.

'I never had a dog,' said Arturo, looking over his shoulder into the back seat. 'She seems very good.'

'I never had a dog either,' said Darcy. 'But when we were younger our gran had a dog, and we helped with the next-door neighbour's dog too. I'm not too sure I would have remembered everything about training a puppy.'

She started to look a bit nervous as they approached the cottage. 'Do you think she'll like it?'

He couldn't help but be amused by her worry. 'I think she'll love it. Do you think it's a good idea taking her back and forth between here and the kennel?'

Darcy frowned as they pulled up at her door. 'I'm not sure, but I *am* sure the rescue place know what they are doing. Maybe they're scared she'll be overwhelmed. Or maybe it's me they're actually keeping an eye on, and not Ruby.'

'I wouldn't be at all surprised,' he admitted,

getting out of the car and walking around to help retrieve all the items from the boot. 'She's been in the shelter for three years. Maybe that's got something to do with it. Maybe it's a harder adjustment for a dog that's been there a while.'

Darcy opened the back driver's door and couldn't hide her smile as Ruby jumped down and sniffed the air around her.

'If it's possible,' murmured Arturo, 'I think she's a bit confused.'

'She will be, if she's always been a city dog,' said Darcy. 'She'll be smelling the sheep, cows and horses from the farm nearby. I did warn my neighbour I was getting a dog—just in case there were any issues.'

She'd told the farmer. She'd told her neighbour, but she hadn't managed to have that conversation with him.

'Dogs aren't supposed to be on farm land, are they?'

'Not unless they belong to the farmer, or are on a lead,' said Darcy, still watching Ruby smell the air.

She opened her front door as Arturo approached with the bed and food. 'C'mon Ruby, come and have a look inside to see what you think.'

Arturo watched in fascination as Darcy put out some food, just like Jen had told her to, and set up the bed for Ruby. He'd never imagined Darcy having a maternal side, but it seemed he'd completely missed it. Even if her maternal side only came out for dogs.

Ruby had a good sniff around the cottage, making herself at home, eating some food, drinking some water, then licking the glass wall.

Arturo had settled on the sofa, Darcy beside him as they watched Ruby. 'I can live with smears,' she said as she put her head on his shoulder. Ruby turned at her voice, came over, looked at them both, then jumped up on the sofa, sprawling herself across them.

They couldn't help but laugh, rubbing her head and patting her belly, and watching the dark red dog hairs coat the space around them.

'Going to need to get a better vacuum cleaner,' Darcy sighed, but the smile was still wide.

'So,' Arturo started gently, 'the commitment side—it doesn't bother you?'

She took a moment, opened her mouth and then just smiled. 'It's supposed to, isn't it?' Her eyes were wide as she turned to Arturo. 'But...' She shook her head. 'For the strangest reason, it just doesn't.' Her brow wrinkled, 'I mean, if you'd suggested this to me a few weeks ago— or put this down on paper for me—I would have been horrified.'

'So, what's changed?'

He had to ask, because it was clearer and clearer to him that he had to find out where he could fit into Darcy's life. *If* he could fit into Darcy's life.

She took in a shaky breath and looked at Arturo. 'I guess, in the space of a few weeks, a lot of things have changed.'

'Because of your sister's bucket list?'

'I guess so,' she said reluctantly. 'Or maybe it was just the right time.' She sighed. 'The right time for everything. To look at my life. To decide why I was where I was. To let something like a bucket list push me out of my comfort zone.'

'Am I out of your comfort zone?' He wasn't sure what he wanted the answer to this question to be. 'I have to be honest. I kind of hoped when you'd looked at the commitment thing on your bucket list, you might have considered something other than a dog.'

Her mouth dropped open. She continued stroking Ruby, almost using her as a comfort blanket. 'Honestly? You are? You terrify me.'

There. She'd said it. Was this his cue to make a graceful retreat and say nothing?

He shook his head. 'I'd hoped… I'd hoped that once we got back home, we would have a chance to talk. To see what we wanted to happen next.'

Darcy closed her eyes for a second. 'But you've been gone the last few days.'

He cringed inwardly. 'I have. I was taking care of one last job.'

'What do you mean, one last job?'

He chose his words carefully. 'My job really isn't conducive to having a relationship with someone. I had one last thing to see through—something that my father had sought for many years. I've finally managed to return it to the rightful owners.'

She looked at him carefully. 'I would never ask you to give up a job that you love.'

'I know that.'

But the look in her gaze was panicked. 'We've only known each other a few weeks. How can you make a decision like that?' She put her hand to her chest. 'Based on me? Based on having a relationship with me that we've not even discussed yet?'

'Should I have waited?' Now he was feeling panicked. Maybe he hadn't thought this through.

She threw up her hands and Ruby jerked. So she placed them back carefully, and spoke in a low voice. 'I told you I hadn't been to a wedding in a while. It was…difficult.'

'It didn't seem difficult when we were in bed together, or did I miss something?'

As soon as the words were out of his mouth, he regretted them.

She flinched.

'Was it difficult because you realised you're still in love with your ex?' He was angry now, but kept it from his voice. He wanted to know why Darcy didn't seem as dedicated to this relationship as he was.

She shook her head. 'I'm not. But it gave me a chance to reconsider a number of things. Including the part I played in our wedding not taking place.' She kept shaking her head. 'I'd never done that before. I'd just moved on. Not wasted too much time thinking about it.' Now she met his gaze. 'Shouldn't that have partly told me what I needed to know?'

And now she'd started talking it seemed as if she didn't want to stop. 'You know the part that gripped me most about your sister's wedding?'

'What?'

'The way Dante and Cara looked at each other...' She brought her clenched hand up to her heart and shook her head. 'I would never have looked at Damian like that, nor he me.'

Tears were trickling down her face. Damian. Arturo even hated the name. 'Your sister's wedding was beautiful. But I probably shouldn't have come. The last thing I wanted to do was spoil things for you because I was facing up to what I should have, years ago.'

That made his heart clench further. The last thing he wanted was her to feel guilt.

'But it also made me face up to a whole lot more.'

'Like what?'

'Like I don't know if I'm ever going to be ready for a happy ever after. How can I, when I constantly think that my sister can't?' Her voice was shaky now. 'When all your relatives started talking to me, wanting to know everything about me, wanting to know if I'd be the next Mrs Fabiano, I just felt swamped. Just like when I saw your family home. I don't mix in those circles. I never have. How can I do it now? I don't even speak the language. How could we even contemplate having a relationship when we are so far apart?'

'Money isn't everything,' he said quietly.

She sucked in a deep breath. 'I know,' she agreed. 'But look at us, Arturo. Look at where we are. You have a job that's dangerous. You deliberately live far from home. I get the impression you haven't had much at stake in your life before this—' the tears were really flowing now '—and that's wrong. So wrong.'

'I didn't have anything to live for before,' he

said quietly, and he realised that he actually meant it.

Another tear streaked down her cheek. 'You have so much to live for, Arturo. You're wonderful. But you need to realise that for yourself.'

She rested her hand on Ruby again, giving her a gentle pat. 'This?' she said. 'This is about as much as I can do right now. This is where I feel as if I can be safe. I know she'll break my heart in a few years, but I'll be ready for that.' She looked at him with tear-filled eyes. 'I'll make sure I am.'

This was all going so wrong for Arturo. He wanted to wind the clock back a few weeks— when they were sitting in the bar at the hotel, flirting, and everything was shiny and new.

There was silence for a few moments, then Arturo stood. It was the only thing he could do right now because his heart was breaking. 'Things have moved quickly between us,' he started.

'Too quickly,' she interrupted.

He hated the fact he was saying these words. He wished none of this was true. But if he really loved Darcy, if he really wanted what was best for her, he had to put her needs first, and put his own feelings aside.

'This isn't the way things are meant to be,' said Arturo softly. 'This isn't the way I want things to be between us. I love you, Darcy. I'm not sure when, or where, but at some point in the last few weeks I've met someone who's made me question choices in my life. Who has made me look at myself and let me know that I need to make changes to move on with my life.'

He took another breath. 'But I can't solve everything. You need to believe that you're worthy of a happy ever after, Darcy. You need to believe it, and reach out and grab it.'

When she didn't answer, he knew he had no other option available.

'I'm sorry it's come to this,' he said, hearing his own voice crack. He wanted to fix this. He wanted to make everything okay. He wanted more than anything to make his relationship with Darcy work.

But she didn't want that. And even though it was breaking his heart, he loved and respected her enough to put her wishes before his.

'Good luck with Ruby. She's found a wonderful owner.'

Darcy tilted her chin upwards. 'I think she's found me.'

And with a final nod he turned and headed out of the door. Out into his own car, away from the cottage in the country that held his person, and his heart.

CHAPTER SEVENTEEN

NOTHING HURT AS much as this. Not the acknowledgement that some of the things Arturo had said to her were true, and not the fact that she finally had to face up to her own truths. Her own life.

She'd been hiding away for the last five years.

The bucket list had been the kick in the butt that she'd needed badly. It had pushed her out of her comfort zone and made her examine her life. How could Laura have been so insightful five years ago?

Because at the end of the day, that was what all this came down to. Laura.

Darcy had shut herself off from the majority of her friends and family in an illusion of getting on with her new working life and buying and renovating a house.

All of it was the ultimate act of avoidance. While she avoided her parents and her sister, she was away from everything that reminded her of Laura. Part of the triggers of the wedding had been around the fact it was the last major event she'd attended with her sister.

It wasn't around Damian. It had never been about Damian. It was about remembering Laura in her bridesmaid dress. Remembering the paleness of her skin, and the way she'd trembled while they all waited. It was about the fact she'd fled for five days to Edinburgh and had felt horribly guilty about that ever since.

It didn't matter that Fizz and her parents had been with Laura those five days. It was because when she'd returned five days later Laura had looked worse than ever. And in those final two months she'd had to deal with putting a house on the market and packing it up, rather than spending every minute with her sister.

She knew that none of her family blamed her in any way. But she blamed herself. And even though she'd allowed that to beat herself up, and consume her with guilt, it meant that she didn't need to concentrate on the other part.

The part that told her Laura had contracted a horrible disease that couldn't be cured and there was nothing that she or anyone else could have done about it.

Accepting that would have meant eventually moving on. It would mean stopping thinking of every single thing Laura had missed out on.

Accepting that would mean realising that she *was* worthy of a happy ever after. Arturo had seen it more clearly than she had.

And moving on was the plan that her sister had for her.

It seemed it was time to decide if that was the plan she had for herself.

CHAPTER EIGHTEEN

IT HAD BEEN five days, and Arturo couldn't bear it a second longer. The more he thought things through and processed, the more he came up with a million other ways he could have handled it and sorted things between them.

He wanted to see Darcy. He wanted to phone her or message her or go to her house, but he wasn't sure how she felt. And that made his heart ache.

After days of pacing, he finally decided to take the bull by the horns and try a neutral venue.

Jen looked up in surprise as he walked into the rescue centre. He gave her a cautious smile. 'I came to see if Darcy was here to pick up Ruby.'

She frowned slightly. 'She changed her day. She had her yesterday, and Ruby's going home day is on Sunday.'

He swallowed, thrown for a few seconds by the change of plan. 'Did she say why she had to change?' he ventured.

It seemed that Jen took pity on him. 'Something about a bucket list. The last thing on it.'

His skin prickled. The last instruction on the bucket list.

Find somewhere peaceful...to reflect on what you want out of life.

But where would Darcy go? Did she have somewhere in her home town of Bath that she'd consider a place to contemplate the world? Or maybe some place she'd gone with Laura? He tried to think of anywhere in Edinburgh. But there could be a million places. Up at Arthur's Seat with a view of the city. The Royal Botanic Gardens or the Princes Street Gardens. Maybe even a trip to Rosslyn Chapel. It could be any of them.

He was feeling desperate now. 'Did she happen to say where she was going?'

Jen gave him a sympathetic look. 'Something about returning to a place. I think she said it was in Rome.'

He froze. 'Rome?'

She nodded. 'She said she'd definitely be back for Sunday and couldn't wait to take Ruby home permanently.'

Every beat of his heart was pumping the blood around his body more quickly, an adrenaline response for what he had to do next. There was no question about it. If he didn't do this, he would regret it for the rest of his life—because that would be a life without Darcy in it.

And he didn't want to accept that, not without taking that one final step.

CHAPTER NINETEEN

It was a totally different experience being here alone.

It didn't help that it was the middle of the night. And while the Trevi Fountain wasn't exactly quiet, it wasn't busy either. It was two in the morning, and there were a few late-night stragglers, and some tourists who'd obviously heard of the best time to visit.

Once the taxi had dropped her, she'd taken a short walk to the place they'd bought carryout coffee and cake, then taken it back along to the night-lit fountain, which was every bit as stunning as it had been a few weeks ago.

But her heart didn't sit quite right.

She settled on the steps and looked up at the star-filled sky. 'Okay then, Laura. You've got me questioning what I want out of life. Is there a right answer to this question, or can I sit here and tell you that I still don't know?'

She dropped her head as she said those words

because she knew that wasn't true. Her heart was telling her exactly what she wanted. But the steps were just too far.

As a few more people moved away she stood up and went closer to the fountain, taking a coin from her pocket. She'd already made one wish here, and it seemed like she might have blown that one.

Was it really worth making another?

She closed her eyes and spun around, ready to throw the coin over her shoulder, but her spinning was off-centre and she knocked right into someone.

'Sorry!' she exclaimed, opening her eyes then catching her breath in shock.

Arturo did not look his usual suave and calm self. His hair was out of place, his cheeks slightly red and his jacket and shirt crumpled. He was a bit out of breath. Had he been running?

'You weren't here,' he started. 'I thought I'd got it wrong. I was about to go to the Colosseum instead.' He caught sight of the paper coffee cup and bag sitting on the steps just in front of them, and he obviously realised where she'd been.

'Oh.'

'We must have crossed paths,' she said, her voice shaky.

'That could have been a disaster,' he replied, his brown eyes fixed on hers.

There was silence for a few moments then they both started at once.

'I needed to see you again.'

'I wanted to see you.'

They both paused, looking at each other in the pale light.

'You speak,' he said.

She took a breath. 'Arturo, this wasn't ever really about us. This was about me. And learning that I have to move on. I've spent so long thinking I don't really deserve to. That Laura was cheated out of so much. That so many of the experiences I'll have now should have been experienced by her too. I haven't been able to move on for fear of leaving my sister behind. I guess I've spent most of my time worrying about losing someone else.'

She put her hand up to her chest. 'I lost an ex—who wasn't worth much—then I lost my sister. Part of me thinks I must have deserved all this. Building the pieces of my heart back together has been the hardest thing I've ever done. And I don't know if I can put myself in a position where I might have to do that again. Trying to convince myself that I'm worthy of a second chance is hard.'

He gave a solemn nod. 'And us?'

She gave a gentle smile, reached up and touched the side of his cheek. 'We just got caught in the crossfire. My sister gave me a bucket list to teach me to live again. I got the pleasure of doing that with you.'

He caught her hand in his, holding it next to his cheek. 'I love you, Darcy. I never expected to. I don't even know if I'm supposed to. All I know is that, from the moment I met you, we've connected in a way I've never felt before.'

She blinked, feeling tears brim in her eyes. 'And I love you too, Arturo. I've never met anyone like you. I've learned to dance, had a whistlestop tour of Rome. I've been to an incredible family wedding and picked a wonderful dog. You've given me the best memories possible.'

'But...?' he asked, his voice wary.

'But,' she said as some tears started to fall, 'what if I lose you too? What if I take a chance on you, on us, and it doesn't work out? What if I get left again, and this time I don't have the strength to put the pieces of my heart back together?'

He gave her the gentlest smile as he reached up and cupped her cheek. 'We are more alike than you know.' He gave a shake of his head. 'When I lost my father, and my fiancée, I thought that was it. My life didn't mean much any more. Of course I love my mother and sister, but I've always known that, deep down, they would survive if I wasn't around. I never found anyone else to invest in—to take a chance on. Until I met you.'

He smiled at her. 'How could I have a proper relationship when I moved around all the time? I thought if I didn't tread the same path as my father I would be letting him down.' His brow furrowed. 'But now I try and be reflective about it, I realise that the man I loved was actually selfish. He put my mother through heartache. He put his family at risk. I need to get over that. I need to move beyond that.'

Something inside her twisted. 'You said that you were changing your job. I didn't want you to do that for me.'

He moved his flat hand to his chest. 'And I'm not. I'm doing it for *me*. I'll still do what I love. Archaeology. I may have spells where I need to be away on digs. I'll likely work with museums around the world. But nothing that could bring anyone harm. I needed to see the big picture. Cara's wedding helped me do that. I'm sorry you were overwhelmed by my relatives. They love you. They want me to be happy—and they could see that I was happy—with you.'

He moved her over to the steps, where they could both sit down. 'But changing my job is only a tiny part of this,' he said seriously.

'Okay,' she agreed, wondering what would come next.

'It's about you and me. Are we both ready for this? Are we both ready for a relationship? Are we ready to take a second chance—on each other?'

He put one hand on his heart. 'I love you. I know I love you. But I think, in different ways, both of us have been in a bubble of grief for the last few years, processing differently, and dealing with things in our own way. I want this to work. I want *us* to work. And I think we might stand the best chance if we maybe ask for some help.'

She blinked as a huge lump appeared at the back of her throat. He saw her. He knew her. And he still wanted to be here.

'I love you too,' she said. 'I didn't expect to. But the connection? I feel it too, more than anything. And whilst I hate what you're saying, in a way, I know it needs to be said. Our family were all offered counselling just after Laura died. My mum and dad went, but Fizz and I didn't. I think it's time for me to take up the offer. To learn how to move on without her, and not to feel guilty about it. And to learn how to have a relationship with my sister without feeling as though something is missing. To know that I am worthy of being happy. To learn that we can be enough on our own. And, most of all—' she took the biggest breath '—to take a chance on someone else. To reach out and grab the happiness that's right in front of me. To learn to not be afraid.'

He leaned forward and kissed her head. 'I don't ever want you to be afraid, Darcy. I promise you that your heart is safe with me.'

She mirrored his pose and put her hand up to her heart. 'How do you feel about agreeing that while we work on it we can still be together?'

He slid his hand into hers. 'I can't think of anything I want more. Your bucket list was fate, Darcy. For you, and for me. We can do this—we can do this together.'

She tilted her mouth up towards his. 'There's nothing I want more.'

He grinned and whispered in her ear, 'Then maybe we can create our own bucket list.'

'That will be negotiable,' she agreed. And then she kissed him at the most magical fountain in the world, tossing a coin over both their shoulders, because she wanted to start the way she meant to continue.

EPILOGUE

One year later

'READY?' FIZZ ASKED her sister.

'Absolutely.' Darcy grinned, picking up her colourful wedding bouquet and heading to the top of the stairs.

Although it would have been lovely to get married at Arturo's Italian estate, the complications involved in taking Ruby with them were more than either wanted. Ruby was getting older, and neither wanted to put strain on their guest of honour at their wedding.

Arturo, with the help of his sister, had found a beautiful Scottish castle to hire for the event and, from the sounds outside, the guests were already having a ball.

'Okay?' checked Fizz one more time.

Darcy nodded, and picked up the skirts of her wedding dress to start down the stairs. Her relationship with her sister was so much more solid now. In the last year they'd talked every day and seen each other a dozen times.

Her dad was waiting for her at the bottom of the stairs. He looked totally relaxed, and she knew he wouldn't have been able to resist checking that Arturo was already in place.

She'd never had a single doubt about her and Arturo. They'd spent the last year doing some individual counselling, then some together. Grief was a journey. And they were walking the path together.

As Darcy and her father stepped outside, the bright Scottish sun was high in the air. The temperature was every bit as warm in Scotland today as it was in Italy. 'This is clearly our one week of summer,' whispered her dad in her ear as he gave a little tug at his collar.

The ceremony was being held in the grounds of the castle, and as she looked down the aisle she could see her gorgeous groom waiting for her. Arturo was so handsome in his wedding suit and bow tie, and her heart swelled in her chest.

She practically wanted to skip down the aisle, but she let Fizz walk in front of her, nodding at her own beau as she went, then Darcy and her father walked down the rose-strewn aisle.

Whilst her father nodded at their guests, Darcy only had eyes for her groom. As they reached the front he bent forward and whispered in her ear. 'You look stunning.'

She couldn't stop smiling. Her dress had incorporated some Italian lace to pay homage to her new family and she'd had fun choosing it with her mum, sister, Cara and Arturo's mother.

They both turned to watch Ruby, with the rings tied around her neck, come towards them. Her joints had been giving her issues and she had developed a limp, but to Darcy and Arturo she just represented love. Arturo bent down, gave her a treat, a kiss on her head, and untied the rings. Ruby sat proudly at their feet.

The celebrant started the ceremony and it passed in a blur for Darcy, as they sang some songs of celebration and exchanged rings.

As the celebrant announced them man and wife, Arturo settled his hands on his hips. He couldn't stop smiling. 'Well, my Bucket List Bride,' he said, 'how about we seal this with a kiss?'

Then he caught her and tipped her backwards, recreating their kiss from a year before as their guests shouted and Ruby barked in celebration.

* * * * *

Look out for the next story in
The Life-Changing List duet

A Fake Bride's Guide to Forever
by Kate Hardy

And if you enjoyed this story,
check out these other great reads from
Scarlet Wilson

Cinderella's Costa Rican Adventure
Cinderella's New York Christmas
The Italian Billionaire's New Year Bride

All available now!